STRIPE LEFT

PARANORMAL DATING AGENCY
BOOK 67

MILLY TAIDEN

STRIPE LEFT
PARANORMAL DATING AGENCY

NEW YORK TIMES and USA TODAY BESTSELLING AUTHOR
MILLY TAIDEN

This book is a work of fiction. The names, characters, places, and incidents are fictitious or have been used fictitiously, and are not to be construed as real in any way. Any resemblance to persons, living or dead, actual events, locales, or organizations is entirely coincidental.

Published By
Latin Goddess Press
Winter Springs, FL 32708
http://millytaiden.com
Bearly Marked
Copyright © 2023 by Milly Taiden
Cover: Willsin Rowe
All Rights Are Reserved. No part of this book may be used or reproduced in any manner whatsoever without written permission, except in the case of brief quotations embodied in critical articles and reviews.
Property of Milly Taiden
January 2023

❋ Created with Vellum

ABOUT THE BOOK

Allie Varga, a tiger shifter, left the luxuries of her parents' home to make it on her own. No one was going to tell her how to live her life. So when she met her fated mate, her decision to solidify the bond thrilled her. **But her parents weren't so happy, and they were powerful people in the community. Powerful enough to wipe away her entire life.**

Marc Romero, a tiger firefighter, grew up in a working-class family. He is proud of the life he's built and even prouder that his mate accepts him for who he is. **His future with his mate looks amazing until she goes to her**

parents' home and comes out no longer knowing who he is.

How can she not remember him? Fated mates are joined in their souls. Only with Gerri's help can Marc discover the horrific acts that Allie's parents inflict on her. **And then, how can he possibly bring back to her what's been destroyed?**

—For my lovely readers.

Thank you for reading.

ONE

ALLIE

"Ms. Varga?" the woman asked as she opened the door for Allie.

"Yep! That's me!" Allie made her way into the office and glanced around at the spacious interior of The Paranormal Dating Agency. Her stomach did a few flip-flops, thanks to the anxiety wreaking havoc on her mind and body.

She didn't know why she was so damn nervous, but she was. It wasn't that the woman looked unfriendly or anything. Actually, she was a natural beauty. The problem was the scents that Allie had picked up the second she'd walked through the office door. They bombarded her senses, sending her into a tailspin.

"Have a seat. I won't bite," the woman said with a laugh.

"Thanks." Allie pulled out a chair and sat as the woman had suggested. She tried to relax by sucking in a few deep breaths, but that didn't help. It only sent her anxiety to a higher level and made her feel like she was going to pass out.

"I'm Gerri Wilder. It's nice to meet you." The woman took a seat across from her and smiled, making her feel welcome and thankfully stemming the unease that rushed through her.

Allie smiled back. "Sorry, I'm so nervous. I've never done anything like this before," she explained. "Plus, the scent in here is heavy from other shifters. It reminds me of being in a crowd ... surrounded if you will."

It was the strangest collection of scents she had ever picked up in the same room. Sure, her parents had hosted plenty of parties when she had been growing up, but never had her home had this collection of shifters.

"Relax. There's nothing to be nervous about. It's just the two of us, nothing to concern yourself with at all. Now, tell me, what it is that you're looking for? And be honest about it, or it does us no good," Gerri said.

Allie thought for a moment. Why the hell was she here in the first place? What was it she really wanted? Hot sex? Absolutely. Hot sex on a regular basis? Was there some sort of sign-up sheet for that? A sexy guy who she had a hard time keeping her hands off of? Uhh ... hell yes!

Of course, she wanted all that, but she also wanted a best friend. Someone who would love and cherish her. Someone who would treat her like a queen. She was tired of dealing with dickwads who thought they were God's gift to women.

She was especially tired of men who talked big dick games only to have a pecker that was no bigger than her pinkie finger. The whole situation had become depressing and tiresome. And for the love of God, she didn't even want to talk about her mother's attempts to set her up with every eligible bachelor she knew. That was a hard no and even a harder pass. Hence, her meeting with Gerri Wilder, the infamous matchmaker.

"Honestly, I'm not sure what I'm looking for. I'm tired of chasing my tail when it comes to men. The dating world these days is a complete drag. It's exhausting. I just want to find someone like me. Preferably the same species. I've dated a few wolves and other shifters, and while it was fun for a short time, I've found they have no idea what to do with someone like me. I'm not a pack animal. I prefer the solidarity of peace and quiet. Of nights spent with a loved one. No distractions."

"So, you're basically looking for your mate?" Gerri asked with an arched eyebrow.

"I'm not sure I believe in that whole love-at-first-sight or scent thing. My parents had an arranged marriage, and it worked out fine for them. They never once complained about not finding their mate or anything like that. My mom told me they eventually learned to love one another and have always had a great marriage." Allie sighed, thinking about the relationship her parents had.

"Everyone has a true mate out there. You just have to find that one special person."

"If you say so." Allie left it at that. How could she agree or disagree when she didn't buy into that fantasy of one true mate? She had always believed that a person had many great loves over different periods in their lives. Each was solely dependent upon where you were in your maturity and the stage of your life.

"I know exactly who you are looking for. Leave it to me. I'll be in touch with you shortly," Gerri said and stood, ready to show her out.

"Okay. Umm, thanks." Allie stood and headed for the door, thinking that it had been the weirdest, shortest meeting in the history of meetings. She also had zero freaking idea how Gerri was a great matchmaker when she didn't even bother to have her fill out any forms.

There wasn't a single question about what she wanted in a man or what type of men interested her. Just a ... I got it, goodbye. She was so confused, but she shrugged it off, determined to get on with her day.

Allie climbed into her truck and wondered again what the hell had just happened. Had she insulted Gerri? Or were The Paranormal Dating Agency and Gerri Wilder nothing but a damn scam? There was no way that Gerri knew who she was looking for or what she wanted in a man. Not after that short-ass meeting.

Allie was going to have a serious talk with the friends who had sworn Gerri was all that and a bag of chips. They were absolutely full of it, and she freaking knew it.

Allie pulled into her garage and turned her truck off. Normally, she would hop out and dash into her home, but not today. Her mind was in shambles after her meeting with Gerri. She had gone into the meeting optimistic, but that had faded quicker than she could blink.

"I knew I shouldn't have gotten my hopes up," she said out loud.

Her beast sighed in her mind. Allie felt the bite in her animal's sadness as swiftly as she had felt her own. The fact was that despite her best intentions, she had gotten the idea that finding their mate would come easily. Her friends had raved about Gerri's talent and her ability when it came to finding someone's true match.

"I can't believe I put on a bra for that. What a waste of makeup," Allie said, making her way into her house and dropping her purse on the kitchen table. She padded back to her bedroom, unhooked her bra, and flung it on the recliner in the corner.

Grabbing a box of leftover pizza from the fridge, she popped open the lid and threw a couple of slices on a plate. It wasn't as gooey as it was last night when it had been fresh and hot, but whatever. It was good enough for dinner since she didn't feel like cooking.

I'm getting really sick of old pizza, her animal said in her mind.

"Too bad. I'm not cooking. This is as good as it's going to get. At least it's a meat lover's pizza."

True. Better than that rabbit food you love so damn much that it makes me want to hurl. Now, if I were a rabbit, I'd be down with that.

"Eww, hush! Or we're gonna starve tonight if you pop another one of those images up in my head while I'm trying to eat."

Whatever. We spend far too much time denying who we really are. When's the last time I got to take over and run? Spend the day doing what I want? Her animal complained.

"I get it. I do, but there's not really anywhere we can just go and run. It's not like our species is native to this area. It would be hard to keep a huge Siberian tiger hidden. It's not something the locals see running around here on a regular basis."

Fine! Her animal sighed.

"Maybe we can go away for a couple of days. Take a trip up to the mountains or something. That way, you can spend some time out in the wild. I think we're well past the need for it."

Do you really mean it?

"I do. Now, let's choke down this pizza and grab some sleep. We'll leave first thing in the morning since I'm off work for the next two days."

For the first time in months, Allie would put

her stress and worries behind her and take the time she needed for her own mental health.

Allie's phone dinged. She glanced down at the incoming call.

"Well, well, well," she said, wondering why Gerri was calling. "Hello," she answered the call.

"Hi, Allie. I wanted to see if you were available for a date tomorrow night. I have someone you'll love to meet."

"Can you tell me more about him?" Allie asked, feeling hopeful for the first time since she'd left her office.

"Actually, I'd rather you just meet him and see what you think," Gerri said.

"Oh." Her hope quickly faded. "Can it wait? I'm leaving first thing in the morning to go camping for a few days. I've been dying to decompress and stretch my legs. I'm sure you understand." Allie hoped she didn't upset Gerri with her answer. But what the hell? If he was her true mate, he'd wait for her. If not. Oh, well.

"Oh, how fun! Where are you off to?" Gerri asked.

"Moonheart Lake."

"That's such a beautiful area and a great place

to escape to. Just text or call me when you get back."

"I will. Thanks."

"Have a good time. Talk soon," Gerri said and ended the call.

Allie looked down at her phone once more, confused by her second conversation with Gerri. It wasn't that Gerri had been rude or anything. She'd just seemed cryptic. To say the least.

"Whatever." Allie let it go and continued with her plans to spend the weekend at Moonheart Lake. She'd deal with Gerri and the date she wanted her to go on when she got back.

TWO

MARC

Marc Romero drove like a bat out of hell to make it to the spot in time. His friend Gerri had given him the lowdown on a woman who may be of interest to him. Not just *of interest*, she might actually be *the one*. Well, that was what Gerri had told him anyway. He just hadn't wanted to get his hopes up. Yeah, right! His hopes were higher than a 747 at cruising altitude.

The whole idea of finding his mate had him chasing his damn tail. It had been years since he'd heard of a single female like him. Most female tigers lived in close, tight-knit communities where they often subscribed to arranged marriages. Those people were something else altogether.

He'd tried like hell to fit in with their community, but they wanted doctors and lawyers. Not blue-collared workers and definitely not someone who fights fires for a living. To people like that, he'd been considered insane right off the bat.

It wasn't that he had anything against doctors or lawyers, but that hadn't been his calling. Marc had always wanted to help people. With his size and speed, he had the ability to do so. Saving people in perilous situations and making a difference is what mattered to him. Not that doctors didn't save people. They did, but they didn't run into burning buildings to do their job.

They had looked down on him and his life choices, and that was fine by him. He didn't feel the need to prove himself to any of those uptight SOBs. Sadly, that had meant zero access to his possible mate. That had never set right with him, but there wasn't a damn thing he could do about it.

Gerri had told him not to worry. She would find his mate for him. He had always known that if anyone could find his female, it would be Gerri. Her talents were off the chart when it came to all things in the dating world.

Marc hopped from his truck, closing in on the location Gerri had given him. His animal pressed against him, knowing what the score was. He wanted to be free to search for his mate. Marc undressed, crammed his clothes into a backpack, and then sucked in a deep breath to surrender control to his animal.

He felt each bone crack and break to reform his shape. His face elongated, and fangs pushed through his gums. He welcomed the brief pain of the shift, knowing that he would soon feel the power of his other half coursing through him.

Once his shift was complete, he chuffed and scratched at the grass beneath his paw.

Finally! his tiger said.

"Go. Find her!"

His beast didn't waste a second. After snatching his pack in his jaws, his paws raced across the green grass, running fast and hard until his muscles burned from the exertion. His speed was dizzying as he traversed the hills around the lake, searching for his mate. Once he caught her scent, he sped off in her direction, still unsure as to how he wanted to approach her.

Instead of charging in and scaring her, Marc slowed his pace, wanting to get a glimpse of the woman Gerri assumed to be his mate. He crouched, hiding behind a patch of brush and trees, hoping to remain unseen for the time being. The fact that she was in her human form was probably the only reason she couldn't scent him yet.

The sun peeked through the clouds, highlighting the red streaks in her otherwise dark wavy hair. The crimson highlights looked like flames swirling in the light breeze. Her upturned face sought out the lone ray of sun that had pushed through the darkened sky. A small smile spread across her face.

"Beautiful," he said to his beast.

Mine! his beast replied.

He knew the single word to be true the second it passed through his mind. Gerri had been correct. The beauty was, indeed, his mate.

Her stunning golden eyes caught his attention when her head whipped in his direction. Had he not been crouched already, the full range of her beauty might have very well knocked him to his knees. She was unlike any creature he had ever seen. Her beauty … unmatched by anyone to have walked the earth before her. With long hair flowing nearly to her curvy waist, and legs that seemed to go on forever, Marc wanted to worship the ground she walked on.

When she turned and he got a full-on view of

that perfect ass ... he swore his heart stopped beating. It took every ounce of willpower in his body to keep from charging and pouncing on her. He wanted to feel every one of those luscious curves of hers under him as he pounded into her and made her moan his name.

He watched her every move as she spun on her heel and headed back to her truck. Lifting the truck's bed cover, she pulled out a long rectangular case. She stepped back to survey the area before opening the case and pulling out what looked like a tent.

He was not only surprised but also quite impressed when it came to her efficiency at her task. She worked quickly to set up her little campsite and build a fire. Once she was done putting everything out, she grabbed two chairs from the bed of her truck and set them in front of the fire. She grabbed a beer from the cooler and kicked back in the lounge chair.

"Are you going to keep hiding behind those bushes all day, or are you going to join me?" Her angelic voice carried on the wind to his ears, sending a shock through his system.

Without making the decision to go to her, his feet moved of their own volition.

THREE

ALLIE

Allie took a few sips of her beer, waiting for the voyeur to make his way across the hillside. In his animal form, he was magnificent ... one of the largest males of her species she had seen in a long time. He wasn't someone she knew. She was positive about that. She would have easily remembered a male his size.

And those markings of his ... well, they were something else altogether. Deep, dark orange with jet-black stripes that were perfectly symmetrical covered his body. His striking green eyes captured and held her attention far longer than they should have.

If he looked this damn good in animal form,

she couldn't wait to see what he looked like in his human form. She shivered at the thought.

"So you're the one who's been watching me?" Allie asked as the tiger sauntered closer to her. He was easily twice her size. Maybe she should have been worried about the stranger being so near to her, but she wasn't. There was no menace coming from him, and she knew why. It had taken her a hot minute to realize what *it* was.

Mine! her beast shouted in her mind.

"Mmm-hmm." Allie chewed on her bottom lip, watching very closely as he began his shift from animal to human. The tiny hairs on her arms stood on end as she felt his magic swirling around them.

"Holy shit!" she said to her tiger, sucking in a deep breath. He was easily every inch of six and a half feet with thighs the size of damn tree trunks. Her eyes nearly got stuck on the junk hanging between his legs. Being naked after shifting had its advantages.

She had to tear her glance away and move farther up his body.

Each muscle seemed to flex at the same time as he closed the last bit of distance between them. His close-cropped dark hair framed his chiseled face. His lips were full and puffy and made for kissing.

And that sexy grin of his. Fuck! Her panties would have slid right off her body if she hadn't been sitting.

"I thought I'd been stealthier than that." He glanced away and down at the ground, having the good graces to at least seem embarrassed about his stalkerish behavior.

"You should know better than that." She sniffed. "Just because you can't smell me doesn't mean I can't smell you."

His brows drew down. "What do you mean? I smelled you just fine."

Her fingers went to the chain around her neck. He shouldn't have been able to scent her. Was it because they were fated mates that he could? She needed to talk to her father. She shrugged it off as if it were nothing.

"Care to join me?" she asked, gesturing to the lawn chair beside her.

"Absolutely. So this second chair ... are you expecting someone else, or am I free to take it?"

"It's yours. I always bring an extra chair in case my favorite one breaks. I usually leave it in the back of the truck, but I decided to put it out once I caught your scent, knowing you'd join me at some point. I'm glad I wasn't wrong." Allie decided right then and there that flirting with her would-be mate was perfectly acceptable. After all, she was a female who had needs.

"I was unsure at first, but then I couldn't refuse your invitation once you'd outed me," he said with that sexy-ass grin.

"Well, I figured it would be better to talk to you than to have you creepin' around." Allie shrugged. "Do you want a beer?"

"Sure. Besides, it's kinda required when we're chilling next to a campfire, right?"

"Indeed. So, you got a name?"

"Marc ... Marcus Romero. You?"

"Allie Varga." She handed him a beer.

"Thanks. What brings you up here?"

"I like to get away to stretch my legs. I've found that humans tend to freak out if they see a large tiger running through town."

"Right! All the screaming is ridiculous," he agreed.

"Humans ... such silly creatures." She laughed.

"I agree."

"So, Marc. What brings you all the way up here? Or are you a local?" Allie asked.

"Would you believe me if I told you that I was tipped off by a dating guru?"

"No, way!" Allie gasped. "You're not talking about Gerri Wilder, are you?"

"You know Gerri?" he asked, failing to hide the shock he felt at her response.

"I met with her yesterday." Allie was just as surprised by the turn of events as Marc seemed to be. She wasn't sure what to make of the newest development. She had initially thought that Gerri was a kook, a hack, and was completely and totally full of shit. Now, here she was, fewer than twenty-four hours later, having a conversation with her hotter-than-hell mate ... who just happened to be the same species as she was.

"I've known Gerri for a while. She's been on the lookout for my mate for quite some time. She told me she tried to set up a date for tonight but asked if I could hold off until Monday because you were going out of town. I have to admit, I was so damn curious that I just had to hop in my truck and drive all the way up here just to catch a glimpse of you. I had honestly planned on waiting until Monday to approach you."

"Are you disappointed?" she asked.

"Excuse me?"

"Are you disappointed in what you found?" she asked, quite bluntly, even for her.

"Not at all. In fact, I'm quite impressed so far."

The heat that she'd long forgotten existed rolled through her as Marc eyed her up and down, her nipples pebbling under his heavy stare.

"Is that so?" Her words came out as more of a breathy moan. "Wow. It's getting hot this close to the fire." Allie stood and stepped away from the nearby flames, but she knew that wouldn't cool her down as the heat was coming from within. Flames of desire twisted their way through her body just from her proximity to Marc.

Never before had she wanted to jump on a man and have her way with him. Never had she undressed a man and fucked him raw with her eyes. Geeze! What the hell was wrong with her?

He's our mate. There is nothing wrong with what you are feeling, her tiger said.

Realistically, Allie knew what her animal said was true. Marc was their mate, and her need and want for him was nothing more than pure and raw animal instinct. The human part of her mind was holding her back.

"It's a beautiful day," she said, trying to pull her mind away from how badly she wanted him. She had to get her mind moving in another direction.

"I think I'm looking at someone far more beautiful than the weather."

Marc was suddenly next to her. How he had moved so damn fast without her noticing was nothing short of amazing. Normally, she noticed everything. But her mind had been preoccupied with wanting to jump his bones.

Allie's breath hitched in her throat as she turned to face Marc. His green eyes glowed with desire. She could only imagine that her eyes were doing the same. The heat from his body and his scent enveloped and overwhelmed her.

"You are my beautiful mate." His voice was nothing more than a whisper.

"Yes," she said, not wanting to deny whatever was going on between them. Even if she wanted to deny it, her body wouldn't allow it. She was primed and ready to go despite just meeting him, but that was often the way things worked in their world.

Allie tried to fight that raw need ... the instinct rode her hard, but she couldn't. When it came down to it, she didn't want to. She took a step closer to him. His warm breaths fanned across her face. Damn, his scent was intoxicating as hell.

He lifted his hand to her face and traced two

fingers slowly over the side of her cheek, brushing a few stray hairs out of her face.

"So soft," he breathed.

"Mmm," she said, leaning into his touch. "So warm." She sighed.

"Can I kiss you?" he asked.

"Yes." Anticipation tore through her body. Allie hadn't even thought of uttering the word no. She wanted his lips on hers ... had been imagining those full lips on her since the moment she laid her eyes on him.

FOUR

ALLIE

Before Allie could blink, Marc's lips were on hers. His kiss was soft and tender, exploring every inch of her mouth. His fingers snaked through her hair, holding her tightly to him.

Her arms wrapped around his neck as his tongue met hers, and they began an intimate dance. Passion surged through her veins and headed straight to her core. His free hand worked a path down the small of her back to her ass, clenching her lower cheek in his grasp.

"Oh!" she moaned into his mouth, surprised by how the smallest of touches could set her off.

"I love this ass of yours," he said in between

kisses. He arched his hips against her, pressing his erection against her stomach.

"I ... I," she stammered.

"You don't need to say anything, beautiful. Just tell me if you want me to stop."

Her heart hammered against her ribs. It was do-or-die time. Did she want this to stop? Did she want his kisses and his touches to go away? That was all she had to ask herself.

God, no. She wanted more ... all that he had to offer and then some. It had been so damn long since she had been with a man, and she had never been with someone she wanted with every fiber of her being.

"Don't stop!" she moaned as he kissed a path down her neck and chest, stopping just above the material of her tank top.

His teeth scraped gently over the arches of her breasts, sending goosebumps racing across her skin.

"I want to taste you," Marc said, his voice thick with lust.

As hard as it was for Allie to pull away, that was exactly what she did. Her limbs trembled, and her breaths were just as shaky.

"As much as I want to pull you into my tent and have my way with you, I think we should put the brakes on this for just a moment," she said, motioning to the two of them. She sucked in a deep breath, clearing the sexual fog from her brain.

"What do you suggest we do instead?" he asked.

"Let's go for a run. Down to the lake," she replied.

"That sounds like a great way to cool down." He laughed.

"It does. Race you there." Allie threw her clothes off, shifted, and took off running, needing to get away from Marc before she turned back and tossed him to the ground. Images of her riding his cock flashed through her mind. It took every thread of strength she possessed to keep her feet moving forward toward the lake and away from the hunky man who Gerri had sent to her.

She was going to have sex with him, and the sex would more than likely be life changing, but she just wanted to know a bit about him before they did the no-pants dance. Her tiger wasn't happy with her decision, but it'd just have to deal with it. She had never been one to jump someone's bones without getting to know at least a little bit about them first.

She raced along the well-worn path with Marc

hot on her tail. He was fast, but not quite as fast as her. Giggling like a schoolgirl, she kicked it into high gear and left him in the dust, wanting him to chase her.

A series of chuffs sounded behind her. Marc's frustrations were starting to show. He'd figured he'd be faster because he was the larger of the two, but he was wrong. Allie had always been fast, able to outrun anyone anywhere. Though she wanted to turn and ease his frustrations, she didn't dare because, deep down, she wanted him to work for it. To prove that he was a capable male.

Just when she thought she'd had a good lead on him, she went flying through the air. Marc had pounced on her and held her tightly in his grasp. Quickly shifting back to her human form, Allie let out a loud laugh. Marc growled playfully before shifting back to human as well. He had positioned himself, so he bore the brunt of the force when they hit the ground.

"Gotcha!"

"Color me impressed. I usually outrun everyone. But not you." She smiled down at him. The visions of her riding him rebounded in her mind.

"I'll chase this fine ass to the ends of the earth if

I have to," he said, gripping her ass and dragging her farther up his body until she straddled him.

"Is that so?" She wiggled her hips against him.

"Yes, ma'am. I like you in this position."

"*I* like me in this position. It could be lots and lots of fun." She leaned down and nibbled on his lower lip.

"Could be?" he asked quizzically.

"Yes. When we finally get to that point." She rocked her hips back over his hardened length.

"Mmm. That point ..." he said, latching onto her hips with his hands.

"Yep. That point when I let you slide your rock-hard cock balls deep inside me." Her words were bold as fuck, but she didn't care. They both knew it was only a matter of time before it happened.

"I like the way you think, but I think you should change that previous sentence from *could be* to *will be*. Because I guaran-damn-tee that it will be hella' fun for both of us when I'm pushing myself into you, making you moan for me," he said, lifting his hips off the ground and bucking up.

"I think you could be onto something here. It will, indeed, be fun," she said with a laugh.

"So, what are we waiting for?" he asked.

"I can't just roll over and let you have your way with me. What kind of a woman would I be if I didn't make you at least work for it."

"Ahhh ... so the goal is to get me all hot and bothered."

"Something like that." She smirked. "Now, I think we were going to the lake," she said, jumping off his body and sprinting away on foot this time.

"Frustrating woman." Marc laughed.

FIVE

MARC

Marc had to admit that Gerri had been so right about his mate that it wasn't even funny. The woman was incredible. Damn incredible. The way Allie teased him made him want her more than he'd ever wanted anything in his life. More than he even wanted his next breath or next meal. Since he'd laid his eyes on Allie, his life had flipped on end. Everything he did or said was now about her.

He hadn't been joking when he told her that it would be hella' fun sliding balls deep into her. It was his main mission at this point. Claiming his mate. Yeah, yeah. So what? They had just met. That was the way it worked in the shifter world. He knew his mate the second he had scented her.

Now, thanks to her games, it was all about the chase. He hadn't thought he'd ever catch her in her tiger form, but somehow, he had done just that. Maybe it had been the thrill of the chase, or maybe it had been that he had just wanted her so damn bad. Either way, he'd kicked his ass into high gear, wanting to prove his worth.

When he'd finally caught her and pounced on her, having her in his arms had been pure heaven. When she'd shifted and landed on top of him, a thousand explicit thoughts bounded through his brain. All of them involved them getting naked and her fabulous breasts bouncing up and down as he rammed his cock into her heat.

Now, he was chasing that fine ass of hers again. Fine by him and his beast. It was one game he would play all day if it meant having Allie in his arms again. He had to admit she was quick in both shifter and human form. A lot faster than he'd expected her to be.

The smell of the lake hit him before he turned the final bend on the path. He came to a sudden stop when he saw Allie. Turning to face him, she grinned and walked slowly into the water.

His feet, once again, moved on their own, forcing

him to follow his beautiful mate. With each step, he was mesmerized by her stunning boldness. Every one of her curves was on full display for him, and he appreciated the hell out of it. His cock stood at immediate attention, and now jutted proudly out in front of him as he stepped into the warm water of the lake.

If Allie had been hoping to cool them both off, so to speak, with a swim in the lake, she had seriously underestimated his attraction to her. There would be no shrinkage and no loss of hardness. In fact, he throbbed with need for her ... need for his mate.

"I don't think my plan is working out as well as I thought it would," she said with a smile. Her gaze locked on his cock.

"No. I don't think seeing you naked is going to cool me off any." He palmed his cock and stroked it up and down, imagining that he was sliding himself into his mate.

She chewed on her bottom lip, floating in the water a few feet away from him.

"Does this bother you?" he asked. His voice was thick and heavy with lust.

"Not at all. It's sexy as fuck. I'm actually pretty jealous of your hand right now."

"Feel free to come here and take over if you'd like."

Allie closed the distance between them, quickly swimming to him and standing. He watched in awe as hundreds of tiny droplets of water dripped down her full breasts as she emerged from the water. Wrapping her palm around his cock, he wanted to close his eyes and toss his head back in pleasure, but he didn't. He kept his eyes locked tightly on her.

"Fuck!" he groaned as she worked his cock up and down in her hand.

"You're so thick and hard." Her tongue darted out over her lip.

"It's all for you, beautiful." Marc pulled her closer, wanting skin-on-skin contact.

ALLIE GASPED when their bodies came together. His heat seared her skin and shot straight to her core. She didn't know who she was trying to fool by slowing things down between her and Marc. The chemistry between them was undeniable. Strong. And unlike anything she had ever experienced.

She steadied her hand so it didn't shake when she reached out and stroked his cock. He was so soft, yet so damn hard. She wanted to feel him sliding into her.

His lips closed over hers. Unlike the previous kisses they shared, this kiss was raw and demanding. Demanding that she open up to him, which she did without hesitation. His tongue slipped into her mouth. A soft moan erupted from her and poured into Marc. He gladly swallowed it and coaxed several others from her.

He massaged and kneaded her heavy breasts, tweaking each nipple between his fingers until they were nothing more than hardened peaks. Her body shook with need, her limbs trembling under his touch. For the first time in her life, Allie wondered if a kiss could make her orgasm.

"I can't wait to taste you. I want your honey covering my tongue," Marc growled into her mouth.

"Oh!" she cried out as his hand slipped between her thighs and parted her folds. He quickly found her clit and began a lazy circle around it, making her want him even more.

"I think we need to get out of the water and go somewhere I can take care of you."

"I like that idea," Allie said, tired of fighting the lust she had for him.

Without warning, he scooped her into his arms like she weighed nothing at all. He carried her to a small meadow covered with thick grass and a bounty of wildflowers and laid her down. Hovering above her, he kissed a path between the valley of her breasts and down to her stomach, taking a moment to circle her navel with his tongue.

Her fingers tunneled through his hair as moan after moan flew from her mouth. He pushed her thighs apart with his knees and continued kissing a path toward her core. Allie's back arched off the ground when his tongue slid between her folds and over her clit.

"Oh, God!" She panted for air as he intensified the pressure on her clit, her body quivering beneath him.

Marc wrapped her thighs over his shoulders and dug in, feasting as if she were his personal meal. He licked, kissed, and nibbled with more enthusiasm than she could have ever expected. Propping herself up on her elbows, she watched his every move intently, never taking her eyes from him.

When he glanced up and met her stare, she

was fucking done. Nothing, not a single part of sex, had ever been so fucking hot.

"I need you in me, now!" she demanded, not wanting to wait a moment longer ... no matter how good what he was doing felt. She wanted that hard cock of his slamming into her.

"Patience, beautiful." He slid two fingers into her pussy and scissored them in and out.

"Marc!" Allie cried out, falling back against the ground.

Sucking her clit into his mouth, he continued pumping his fingers, making her shake. The added pressure sent her ass rocketing to the moon. She floated through the expanse of the universe, untethered to anything at all. It was complete bliss. Marc knew how to work her body as no one else had ever been able to.

"God! You taste fucking amazing. I want more. I need to feel you coming all over my cock." Marc positioned himself at her folds. The head of his cock pressed against her entrance, throbbing with anticipation.

"I need you in me. Now! Please, Marc," Allie begged, her body going to implode if she didn't have him right that second.

He plunged deep into her wetness with one

twist of his hips. There was no inching slowly in or giving her time to adjust to his size. "So damn tight," he growled.

"Ohhh!" she cried out at the sudden but welcome intrusion. She had never felt so full in her entire life. The way he stretched her inner walls was the purest and simplest form of pleasure she had ever felt.

"You fit me like a glove. The way your pussy keeps clenching my cock. So fucking good." He groaned, holding perfectly still.

Allie bucked her hips under him, wanting to come so damn hard.

"More!" she demanded. "Please. I need more!" Allie didn't give a fuck how needy she sounded or that she was literally begging him to fuck her. All she wanted was for Marc to slam into her.

"Like this?" He inched out before ramming his cock balls deep into her.

"Fuck! Yes!" she shouted. "That's exactly what I like. What I want."

"Good to know my mate likes it hard because I want nothing more than to hear you screaming my name."

"Then do it. Make me come so fucking hard that I scream for you."

"That sounds like a challenge."

God, that sexy grin of his would be the death of her. Death by pleasure if she had to go anytime soon, that would be the way that she preferred to go out.

"Take it as you like. Just fuck me, please."

"As you wish." Marc pulled back again before ramming back into her, repeating the motion.

Her breasts bounced with each thrust. She arched her back off the ground when he circled her clit with his thumb. The sensations ravaging her body were almost more than she could take. It had been so long since she had been with a man. And never with a man who knew how to work her body like Marc did. He seemed to know exactly what she needed before she did. It was the most incredible thing she'd ever experienced.

"Oh, God! Yes! Just like that!"

He stretched his body out over hers. His mouth crashed into hers. He licked and nibbled at her lips, making love to her mouth just as he sped up his thrusts. Every move he made felt so damn good. The pressure building in her body already had her chasing her next climax.

She wrapped her legs around his waist, locking her ankles together. Her nails dug into his back to the point that she feared she would draw blood. She bucked her hips up and down to meet each of his long hard strokes.

"You are so fucking beautiful," Marc said in between nibbles. "I love the way your pussy feels wrapped so tight around my cock."

"I love the way you feel slamming into me, but I need more. I need you to fuck me harder." She wanted to come so damn bad, and he was keeping her right on the edge of her climax, frustrating the hell out of her.

"Get on your hands and knees," he said, quickly pulling out of her.

"Yes!" she gasped at the emptiness she felt. Allie did as he'd asked and positioned herself for the hard pounding she hoped was coming.

"Such a beautiful full ass. So perfect." Marc's hand swept over her cheeks. His fingers danced a path up her spine and quickly back down to her ass. He palmed his cock and pumped it up and down in his fist before teasing her clit with the head. Sliding it up to her entrance, he pushed the head in and covered it in her juices.

"Mmm," she moaned with anticipation, hoping like hell Marc would slam back into her with the quickness she not only wanted but needed.

"Do you want my cock all the way in?" he asked, slipping out and back down to her clit.

"Please, Marc. Please!" she begged, pushing back against him.

"Why do you want my cock?"

"Because it feels so damn good when you're inside me." That was the absolute truth. His being inside her was unlike anything she had ever felt, and she wanted more.

His palm landed against her ass, and she let out a surprised gasp.

"Ohh!"

"If I didn't know better, I'd say you liked that," he growled.

"Something like that. Now, fuck me!" she commanded.

"You're so sassy. I love it." He rammed his cock in balls deep, pulled back, and repeated the motion.

Allie thought she had died and gone to freaking heaven. The pleasure wreaking havoc on her body was incredible. She pushed back against him, allowing his cock to penetrate her already stuffed pussy even deeper.

"Umm," she moaned, loving the fullness she felt.

Marc grabbed onto her hips and set out at a brutal pace, slamming into her in a repetitive motion, hitting that sweet spot with each thrust. His hips twisted once on the way out and again when he slammed back in, driving her wild.

"I can feel how much you want to come. Let go. Come all over my cock, beautiful." He coaxed her along. Reaching one hand around her waist, his fingers landed on her clit and danced in small circles around the sensitive flesh.

"Yes! Oh!" she cried out as she saw stars. Her second climax rushed through her veins. Her arms and legs shook from the force of Marc's thrusts. If he hadn't been holding on to her, she would have faceplanted into the ground in front of her. Her inner walls clenched again, holding him tight. He had to work to keep his cock inside her.

"God, baby. That's it. I'm going to come with you."

"Yes!" she cried out, gasping for the much-needed air to fill her lungs as his seed shot deep into her.

SIX

ALLIE

"We should probably head back to my camp," Allie said as she looked up at the darkening sky.

"There's a storm on the horizon." Marc didn't like the way the angry clouds were congregating off in the distance.

"I didn't think it was supposed to storm this weekend. Hopefully, it will blow past us."

"I'd much rather have round two with you, right here and now, but I think you're right. We should head back." Marc wanted to throw her down and make her scream his name to the birds. But they should get back before they found themselves out in whatever it was that Mother Nature had planned for them.

"Round two sounds fun, but I need food first. There's a couple of rib eyes in the cooler I planned on making over the fire for dinner."

"Now you're speaking my language," Marc joked. "Are we racing again or just walking?"

"I think we'll be fine walking. It's not too far. Besides, at some point, we're going to actually have to talk." She grinned.

"Talk! Gasp! How dare you suggest such a naughty thing."

"I know, right? It's absolutely scandalous. Well, it would be to my mom." She shrugged, not wanting to think about the implications of meeting her mate on a camping trip. Her mom was going to throw a hissy fit. More than likely her dad, too, but she'd worry about that later. Besides, if Marc was her fated mate, they would have to accept him.

"So, what do you want to know about me?" he asked.

"Well, considering I just slept with you ...."

"You mean fucked my brains out." He grinned and wrapped his hand around hers.

"True. I guess there was no sleeping involved in what we just did. But seriously, I know nothing at all about you other than your name and how well you know how to use that beautiful cock of yours."

The words flew from her mouth before she'd had a chance to stop them. It was no biggie, though. As far as Allie was concerned, two could play the teasing game that he'd started.

"I'm an Aries. I hate the color yellow. My favorite food is steak." Marc shrugged.

"Okay. Not quite what I had in mind, but it's a start." She giggled, completely unsure if he was being serious or not.

"Ask, and I'll tell," he replied, pulling her hand to his mouth and kissing it softly.

"Is this kind of like you show me yours, and I'll show you mine?"

"Well, I've already shown you mine and seen yours ... but sure, why not. We'll go with that."

Allie found herself laughing at Marc's antics. He kept the conversation light which she greatly appreciated.

"Smartass." She laughed.

"Absolutely. If you take life too seriously, it will come back to bite you in the ass, and you'll be miserable. So, I've learned to laugh off as much as I can. It's probably not healthy, and a shrink would more than likely think I'm insane, but it's all good. It works for me."

"I see that. I like it. I've been around too many people lately who just leave me feeling drained after a conversation or any type of interaction at all. I can't deal with all the whining and complaining. It drives me nuts."

"Right. I'm not good with it either. That's why I always try to keep things fun. Sometimes you just have to laugh."

"Right. So, now that we're back to camp. Tell me about you while we get dinner going." Allie added several pieces of wood to the fire and stoked the coals. She wrapped a couple of potatoes in foil and placed them on a pile of hot coals.

"You mean you want to know more than my favorite color and sign?" He smirked.

"Exactly." Allie truly enjoyed their light-hearted banter. It was like nothing she'd ever experienced with a guy. Normally, conversations were awkward and stilted ... not with Marc. Conversations with him were fun and easy ... almost natural.

"Well, I'm a firefighter. I have three older brothers and a younger sister. My parents are great, enjoying their retirement."

"Nice. I always wanted a big family, but my

mother didn't. So, I'm an only child." Allie tried not to let her sadness about her family crop up in her voice. She'd gotten used to being lonely when she was young. Her parents worked high-paying, stress-filled jobs and rarely had time for her. A parade of endless nannies and staff filled her house, raising and taking care of her, and though she had legally been an adult for more than a decade, her parents still kept her on a tight leash.

"What about you? What do you do?" Marc asked.

"I'm a high school teacher."

"Wow. You must have the patience of a saint to deal with all that estrogen and testosterone every day."

"No kidding, but I love my kids. All of them. Some are a handful, but only because they're going through things at home. My heart goes out to all of them, and if I can help them in any way ... well ... that's why I became a teacher."

"So it's safe to say you really like kids?"

"It is. I would love a large family of my own one day." Allie couldn't wait to have the life she'd always wanted ... the family of her dreams filled with lots of kids and a husband who adored her.

"At least we're on the same page when it comes to having a large family."

"That's a good start since we're mates and all." Allie grabbed four steaks from the cooler and seasoned them before tossing them on the rack above the fire. The smell of the meat sizzling made her stomach growl and her mouth water. She'd wished for the tenth time today that she would've eaten breakfast before she left the house.

"Those are some nice-looking cuts of meat. Smells so good."

"I was just thinking the same thing." Allie flipped the steaks over. Flames danced up around them. "Rare or medium rare?"

"Rare."

"Perfect. Makes my job easier, and they taste so much better that way. Can you grab the tray off the table?"

"Sure."

Allie plucked the potatoes from the fire and placed them on the tray that Marc held. Next, she pulled the steaks from the fire.

"You can set them on the picnic table," Allie said, grabbing a bag from a plastic tote in the bed of her truck. She opened the bin and pulled out a small stack of paper plates and silverware. She set them on the table and padded over to the cooler to grab the butter and a couple of bottles of water.

"This looks amazing," Marc said.

"It does. Food cooked over the fire is always the best. It's been so long since I've been up here. I forgot about how much I love everything here. The quiet, the campfires, the ease of cooking a meal. This really is my happy place." Allie glanced around at the view.

"It's stunning here. How often do you make it up this way?"

"I used to come up here every month just to get away and shift. To spend time in the wild, but ..." Allie sighed, not really wanting to discuss why she had stopped coming up.

"I get it. Life gets busy. There are always more important things to take care of."

"Yeah," she answered evasively. "Let's dig in before the food gets cold."

SEVEN

MARC

"I'm so glad the rain blew past us." Allie reclined in her chair and stared at the stars.

"Me too. It's a beautiful night. It's amazing to see so many stars. I don't think I've ever seen this many. At least, not in the city." Marc had never seen anything like it.

Growing up in the city, he was lucky to see a handful now and then. The nighttime sky where he lived was nothing like this. Thousands of tiny diamonds shone brightly in the sky. The small crescent moon served as the perfect backdrop for the twinkling stars.

"I know. It's one of the many reasons I love it here. I would love nothing more than to build a house in the middle of nowhere. I think I'd sit out on the porch every night just to look at the stars."

"That sounds like heaven."

"It's my dream. Honestly," she said. The smile on her face reached from ear to ear.

"So, you want a big house in the middle of nowhere and lots of kids to fill that house?" he asked.

"That sounds about right. Is it too much to ask for?"

"Not at all. It sounds perfect." So perfect, in fact, that Marc started to reconsider his entire life. He thought he'd known what he wanted. The fast-paced city life. The job filled with adrenaline and danger.

Kicking back in front of a fire with his mate, staring up at the stars ... this was exactly what he wanted.

"A penny for your thoughts." Allie laced her fingers around his.

"You're beautiful," he said as he pulled his eyes away from the stars to glance at her.

"That can't be what you were thinking about." She laughed.

Gods, her laugh was beautiful ... like music to

his ears. It calmed his racing heart and soul at the same time.

Mine! his beast shouted in his head for the millionth time.

He ignored his creature. He would not force himself on his mate because of some damn instinct riding him hard.

"I was thinking about how different it is out here versus in the city. How tranquil and soothing it is. I didn't think that by finding my mate, I'd find this level of peace. It's more than I ever expected." Marc had always been a busy person by nature. The tranquility that he felt now that he was with Allie was something altogether new.

"Well, if it's any consolation, I didn't expect to find my mate on this trip. I guess Gerri really came through for both of us."

"It seems too good to be true. Like all this is happening too easily. Life is rarely this easy for me." Though he'd had a loving and happy family as a child, his life had always been tough.

He was the odd boy out at school, towering above all the boys his age. Being dirt poor hadn't helped the situation either. While everyone in his class had the best of the best when it came to clothes and shoes, Marc often dressed in hand-medowns from his older brothers. It never bothered him, but he'd been teased mercilessly for it. His parents had worked hard for everything they'd owned, and he was proud of what he'd had.

"I feel likewise, but at the same time, I think it feels right. We feel right. You can't tell me it doesn't. Besides, we have the fates to thank for bringing us together. Right? Who could fault us for just letting things between us fall into place as the universe intended?"

"Gerri Wilder and the fates." Marc laughed.

"Of course, we can't forget about Gerri. Can I tell you something?" Allie's voice wavered like she was unsure whether she should even bring it up or not.

"Sure. I want you to feel free to tell me whatever is on your mind."

"When I first met Gerri, I thought she was full of shit. She didn't ask a single question about the type of person I was interested in. My meeting with her felt like nothing more than a huge waste of time," Allie laughed. "There! I said it! I'm glad I was wrong about her." She squeezed his hand lightly.

"I'm glad you were wrong too. I've known Gerri for a while, so I knew without a doubt that she would eventually find my mate. You ..." He may have harbored a few doubts, but once he saw Allie, he knew those doubts were nothing but unfounded fears of him spending the rest of his life alone.

"It's been a surprising day," Allie said with a smile.

"Is that a good or bad thing?"

"It's a good thing. Definitely a good thing."

"How about we make it even better?" he asked with a smirk.

"I like the sound of that." Allie laughed as Marc jumped up from his seat and scooped her into his arms.

EIGHT

ALLIE

Allie giggled like a schoolgirl as Marc carried her to the tent. Sure, she had dated strong shifters before, but with Marc, there was something different. Maybe, it was the fact that he was also a tiger, or it could have been that they were fated mates. Hell, it could have been his scent that left her feeling drugged. Either way, being in his arms was unlike anything she had ever experienced.

Setting her on her feet, he unzipped the tent and kicked off his shoes before stepping inside. Allie quickly followed suit and slipped in behind him. The flames from the fire flickered, creating a natural ambiance within the nylon fabric.

Her heart fluttered. Anticipation tore through

her. Even though they had already had sex, she was still nervous, and she didn't know why.

"Easy, gorgeous. There's no reason to be nervous," Marc said, pulling her into his arms.

"I know. It's silly, really. It's not like we haven't done this already." She laid her head on his chest. The rhythmic beats of his heart helped to calm her nerves and anxiety.

His fingers danced gently through her hair and down her shoulder, stopping just above her breasts. "I couldn't have asked for a more beautiful mate." Marc's lips closed over hers. Sweet Jesus, she loved his kisses. They were soft and warm yet demanding. There was no room for negotiation.

She knew exactly what he wanted. In fact, her own body hummed for it. Desired him more than anything else in the world. Her arms wound around his neck. She gasped as his hand traveled over her breast, and her nipples pebbled under his touch.

His tongue darted into her mouth, searching out her tongue. It was almost as if he was making love to her mouth. She moaned into him as his hand slid farther south under her shorts. She pawed at his shirt, pushing it out of the way.

"You have too many clothes on," she moaned.

"That problem has an easy solution." Marc sat up and yanked his shirt over his head, tossing it to the corner of the tent. He shimmied out of his jeans. They quickly followed the same path as his shirt. "Better?" he asked when he lay back down.

"So, so, much better. You're so hot." He really was a beautiful man. Tall and sexy beyond belief. As he lay sprawled out on the sleeping bag, Allie kissed a path down his wide, muscled chest to his stomach. The heat from his body scorched her lips. The head of his cock reached up proudly to his naval.

She ran her tongue over the tip, tasting the drop of precum that had formed. He was sweet and salty, and altogether addictive. Without even thinking about it, her hand wrapped around the base of his cock as her mouth closed over the bulbous head. Pumping her fist up and down his length, she met each of her strokes with her mouth. Up and down, in and out.

"God! That feels amazing," he groaned. His fingers tunneled into her hair.

Allie had never once been turned on by sucking a cock. Never. But when it came to Marc, she could do this all day ... every day. It was just the act of going down on him that turned her on, though. Really, it was enough because his cock was gorgeous. Long and hard and perfectly thick in all the right places.

And it was also his response to her. The way he lifted his hips almost forcing her to take him deeper into her mouth. The way his hand held her head on his cock, encouraging her along. It was seriously fucking hot.

"Baby, you need to stop before you finish me off. There's so much more I want to do with you." Marc pulled her up onto him.

"But I was having fun." Allie pouted. There was no need to pretend anything. She had been enjoying herself more than she should have been.

"You can have more fun later." He continued to slide her up his chest. "Right now, I want your pussy on my face," he growled.

"Mmm. Yes, please!" Allie squatted above Marc's face as he'd requested. Any pouting that had been there disappeared the second his hands wrapped around her hips, and his tongue landed on her clit.

"Fuck! You taste like candy."

She rocked her hips back and forth, making sure he hit all the right spots. When her legs started to shake, and she couldn't take it for another second, she slid down his body until she straddled his cock.

"I want you inside of me," she said before lowering herself down his length.

"But I was having fun," he countered.

"You can have more fun later." She threw his words back at him. "But right now, I think we both need this."

Marc grabbed onto her hips with a punishing grip. "I think you just might be on to something."

"I think you're right. I'm on to something thick, long, and hard, and it feels so fucking good." Allie slid down his length, taking him balls deep inside her. She moaned as she felt her inner walls stretching to the max.

"You're so wet." Marc lifted his hips, pushing his cock deeper into her.

"It's all for you." Allie leaned forward, her hair falling around them. She kissed, licked, and nibbled on his lips as she rocked her hips back and forth, loving the feel of his length sliding in and out of her.

"You feel so fucking good." Marc's eyes glowed from the passion coursing through his veins.

Allie picked up her pace. She leaned back and placed her hands on his knees. Bouncing up and down on his cock, she flew closer and closer to her climax, needing to feel everything Marc had to offer.

"Oh!" she cried out as her inner walls began to clamp down around his length. Eyeing up the side of his neck, she could feel her fangs punching through her gums. The need to claim her mate overshadowed anything else she felt at that moment.

"Make me yours!" Marc turned his head slightly to the side.

As hard as Allie tried to fight the mating instinct, she couldn't. It was too damn strong. Before she had even realized what had happened, she thrust her body forward and struck. Her fangs pushed through the thick skin of his neck like a hot knife through frozen butter. His sweet blood covered her mouth, running down her throat.

Without missing a beat, Marc flipped her over onto her back and began slamming in and out of her. Pulling out to the tip and ramming back in, he sent her flying to the stars. White lights danced in her vision. Surely, the lights had to be from the stars she passed on her way to the heavens.

"Mine!" Marc growled before his fangs

punched through her skin harder than she had expected.

Allie could feel each draw of blood leaving her neck and flowing into her mate's mouth. The simple act of being claimed by her mate sent her surging to unknown heights. She swore her ass had shot straight past heaven and out of the galaxy itself.

NINE

ALLIE

Allie rolled on her side and watched Marc as he slept. Memories of the previous night flashed through her mind, stirring up the now familiar heat for him that had consumed her just hours ago. He looked so peaceful and possibly more handsome than she had remembered when she'd first met him. Or maybe it was because she felt a heat around her chest that she wasn't used to feeling.

She had claimed him as her mate, and he had claimed her. It certainly hadn't been a part of her plans for a relaxing weekend, but it was what it was. She brushed her fingertips over the spot on her neck where he had bitten her to make sure it had been real.

Running her fingers through his hair, she thought about what their future would hold. They had only just met and yet had promised each other a lifetime together with one simple act. A volley of questions ran through Allie's mind. Worry and dread settled in the pit of her stomach when she thought about taking Marc home to meet her family.

She wasn't ashamed of him or anything like that. She worried about what her pretentious family would say or do when they met her new mate. He wasn't a doctor, a lawyer, or a banker. Those were the types of men she had been expected to mate and marry. Not someone who her family would think was below their station.

Hell, her mother had nearly had a coronary when she became a teacher. Her mother had had Allie's entire life planned out from the second she had learned she was pregnant with her. Her mother had even filled out the admissions forms to Harvard and Yale. Of course, she had been accepted to both schools, but she'd turned them down, much to her mother's dismay, to attend a state college known for its teaching program.

Her parents had all but shunned her the day she started her job. While it had sucked, she held firm and continued on with the life that she wanted to live. Not the one her parents thought she should live.

"You look so serious," Marc whispered as his eyes fluttered open. "You're not having second thoughts about our mating, are you?" he asked.

"No. I couldn't be happier about finding you and becoming your mate."

"Then why do you look so conflicted?" Marc rolled over onto his side to face her.

"I'm honestly not conflicted about being your mate. I was thinking about my family and how they are going to react to the fact that I basically ran off for the weekend and mated without them knowing who I've bound myself to.

"They're pretty shady when it comes to who they think is good enough for me, which is silly. But it's always been a point of contention with my parents. You don't worry about anything. I'll deal with them." Allie didn't know how her parents would react, but she'd figure it out when she crossed that bridge.

"So, how are we going to do this?" Allie asked. Would they live together or keep their own places? Did they even live in the same city?

"Good question. I guess we should figure it out,

but first ..." Marc pulled her on top of him. "There's something else we should discuss. It's kind of a hard subject."

"Hmm. It is quite hard." Allie wiggled her hips, teasing him.

"Actually, it's you that needs to be on something."

"Oh, I suppose." Her words dripped with playful sarcasm. Lifting herself up slightly, she wrapped her palm around his cock and positioned it at her entrance. Lowering herself down and letting her pussy swallow every inch of his length.

"Now, that's what I'm talking about." Marc grabbed onto her hips and rocked his pelvis in an upward motion.

"I could wake up to this every day." Allie leaned forward and nibbled on his lips.

"Good, because that's the plan. I don't know how we're ever going to get any work done because if it were up to me, we'd spend all day every day in bed." Marc continued pumping his hips up and down, feeding his cock in and out of her.

"Ohhh, I like the sound of that." And she did. Waking to his cock every morning would be an absolute blessing. She pushed those thoughts aside and concentrated on being in the moment. Rocking her hips, she continued gliding up and down on his length, loving the feeling of his thickness.

"Yeah, you do. And as much as I love you being on top, I need more. I hope that's okay with you?" he said with a wicked grin before flipping her onto her back.

"You're awfully good at the little move." Allie giggled.

"Is that a good or a bad thing?" Marc grinned down at her.

"Oh, I'd say it's a very good thing." Allie wrapped her legs around his back and locked her ankles. "A very good thing, indeed."

"Fuck! I love being inside of you. I love feeling your pussy squeezing my cock so damn tight. It's the best feeling in the world." Marc groaned as he pulled out and rammed back into her sweet sheath.

"Marc! Marc! I'm going to come!" Allie moaned, her nails digging into his back.

"That's it, baby. Come for me. I want to feel you coming all over my cock." He kissed and nipped at her lips, her neck, her breasts ... urging her on.

"Yes! Yes! Yes!" she shouted as her orgasm slammed into her, making her body shake and her limbs tremble.

Marc rode her hard and kept her flying past the moon and into the stars. Just when she thought he'd slow his pace and let her catch her breath, he picked up his speed and began a series of quick, hard thrusts, sending her into back-to-back orgasms.

"Oh! God." Her voice came out as more of a growl than actual words. She felt her eyes glowing and her fangs itching once again.

"You are so damn beautiful when you come like this," Marc growled, pumping his hips once more before his seed burst from his cock and into her.

"Oh, God! That was a fabulous way to wake up." Allie sighed as they lay side by side. For the first time in her existence, she felt calm. A calmness that told her everything would be fine. She sucked in a deep breath, an ear-to-ear smile spreading across her face.

"I'm glad you liked it. So, what's on the agenda for today?"

"Breakfast. Then I'd like to do some hiking before heading home if you're up to it. I wish I could stay up here a few more days, but I have to be back at work in the morning."

"Me too. But we'll figure this all out because

now that I've found you, I have no intention of letting you go. Ever."

"I wouldn't want you to." And that was the absolute truth. Now that Allie had found her mate, she planned on spending the rest of her life with him. They would figure things out as they needed to.

"Good, because you're stuck with me. From now until the end of time." He pulled her close, wrapping her in his arms.

It was becoming her favorite place to be ... in her mate's arms, enveloped by his scent. It truly felt like home.

TEN

ALLIE

The day flew by far faster than Allie had wanted it to. They had spent the day hiking and swimming and doing all the outdoorsy things she loved to do. Thank the heavens Marc was into it as well. They talked and laughed and stopped to make out several times. She'd even managed to snap a few selfies of them together once they'd reached the top of the mountain. Thankfully, the weather had cooperated as well.

Unfortunately, now, she was driving back to her home. She peeked in the rearview mirror to see Marc right behind her. A warmth spread through her chest, and a smile covered her face. She felt almost giddy, like a schoolgirl with her first crush. But it was much more than that.

She had found and claimed her mate. Her life was about to change in ways she'd never imagined. And while she was fine with the thought of change, she wished they had taken a bit of time to hash out some of the details a little better.

For now, he was going to follow her to her house and help her unload. Then, they'd order takeout and go from there. It was scary and exhilarating at the same time.

An hour later, Allie pulled into her driveway. She hit the button for the garage door and pulled in. After hopping out of her truck, she leaned against the tailgate and watched as Marc pulled up to a stop behind her.

God, he really was sexy as fuck. She felt like the luckiest damn girl on the freaking planet, knowing that he was her mate and that she would get to spend the rest of her life with him, doing all the naughty things she wanted to do with him.

"You know we're mated now, right?" Marc grinned at her.

"I do. Where are you going with this?" she asked.

"Well, when you get all worked up and horny, I

can feel it. Not only that, I can smell your desire. So, you can either cool it for a minute while we get your truck unloaded, or we can skip that part and go straight to breaking in your bed." He sauntered up to her and yanked her into his arms. Without saying another word, his mouth closed over hers. The kiss was hot and demanding, and she loved every second of it. His tongue slid into her mouth, and a greedy moan escaped.

He hit the button on the wall to close the garage door and quickly tossed her over his shoulder. "Where's your bedroom?"

"Through the kitchen and turn left." Allie giggled, loving his caveman antics.

Marc turned his head and nipped her playfully on her ass.

"Hey!" she shouted. "Just so you know, payback for that is going to be a bitch."

"Promise?" he laughed.

"Yep. Now, get me to the bedroom and naked."

"Yes, ma'am." Marc turned the corner in the kitchen and headed back to her bedroom.

She squealed when he slapped her ass before setting her on her feet. "You, naked. Now." Allie motioned to Marc. Pulling her tank top over her head and stepping out of her yoga pants and panties. She then tossed them into the basket and padded to the bathroom. Opening the glass enclosure, Allie turned the shower to hot and motioned for Marc to join her.

"I figured we should probably clean up before we get dirty."

"Or we could get dirty while we clean up." He shrugged.

"Oh, I like that idea. A lot." She stepped into the hot spray and moaned. Marc stepped in behind her and pulled her into his arms, his length pressing against her backside. His hands moved up her hips and stomach to her heavy breasts. He tweaked her nipples, turning them into hard peaks with his skilled fingers.

"That's better," he said, spinning her around to face him. His mouth closed over one of her nipples, his teeth scraping lightly over it before moving on to the next. The hot water splashed gently down her back and over her chest. "You look so fucking hot," he growled.

"So do you." She wrapped her fingers around his cock and stroked him up and down, making sure to squeeze gently each time she neared the tip.

"God, I can't wait to be in you."

"Is it always going to be this way? This raw need for one another?" she asked.

"I really hope so because I can't imagine not wanting you. From what I hear, true mates are always like this." He slid a hand down her stomach and began rubbing her mound. Slipping a finger in her pussy, he pumped it in and out.

"Oh! That feels so good." She loved the way he fingered her while rubbing her clit at the same time.

Marc pulled his hand back and quickly spun her around. He placed her hands against the tile wall and pushed her legs apart with his. "I need to be inside of you. I hope that isn't a problem for you." He rubbed his cock up to her tiny back hole. "Have you ever been fucked here?"

"No," she whispered, worried about where this little session would lead them.

"Have you ever thought about it?" He kissed and nibbled on her back, applying the lightest of pressure against her ass.

"I've wondered what it would feel like," she said with a shaky voice. It was something she had always wondered about, but she never had the nerve to ask. The thought of Marc taking her ass both thrilled and scared her. She wasn't quite sure she was ready for it.

"Relax. I'm not going to take your ass now. Right now, I want that sweet wet pussy of yours," he growled before slamming balls deep with one quick shove. "That's what I'm talking about. You're so damn wet for me." He pulled out to the tip and slammed back in.

"Oh, God! Yes! That's exactly what I want. What I need," she purred.

"What's that, baby? My cock in you?"

"It feels so damn good. I think I'm addicted to your cock already. This could be a problem," she admitted.

"Thankfully, that's a problem we can handle." He pulled out to the tip and rocked forward, ramming his cock back into her pussy. His hands wrapped around her hips, holding her tightly. "I have zero issues with giving you as much cock as you need on a daily basis. What kind of mate would I be if I didn't take care of my woman?" He set a steady pace of thrusting in and out.

"Thank God! Because I really think I'm going to want you every moment of every day." Allie didn't know what the hell was going on with her freaking hormones. She had never been so horny in her damn life. Yes, she had always loved sex, but this was different. She had never once felt like she would die without dick. Marc made her feel like that.

"Same, baby. Same. I will never not want you or want to be inside you. You just feel so, so fucking good. I just can't help myself. I want to say it's because we are mates, but it isn't. You are so fucking sexy. So damn beautiful, I just can't seem to help myself. And when I look into those gorgeous eyes of yours, I'm fucking lost." He slammed into her so hard that she nearly lost her footing.

"I think we need to finish up in here and take this into the bedroom, so you can fuck me properly. Not that I don't like this, but I need and want more," she said.

"I agree."

MOMENTS LATER, they were toweled off, and Marc had Allie bent over the bed. He kicked her legs apart, spreading them wider, so he had better access, and plowed his cock as deeply as he could into her.

"Fuck," Marc growled, swearing his eyes rolled clear back into his skull. Nothing had felt as good as being buried balls deep inside his mate. He wasn't lying when he said she was hotter than fucking hell. And with the view he had of her bent over the bed, fuck ... it made him want to come right there and then.

"Marc!" she cried out.

It was music to his ears. He loved hearing Allie moan his name ... total aphrodisiac.

"I love watching your ass bounce up and down every time I slam into you," he growled, feeling his fangs pushing through his gums. "So fucking hot."

"Yes! Yes! Yes!" she shouted.

He held on to her tightly as her body began to vibrate, her pussy clamping down around his cock. He would never tire of this feeling. He would never tire of his cock being inside of her. That was an absolute fact.

He'd held out hope that Gerri would find his mate, but he never expected her to be the total package right out of the gate. Some of his friends had issues with the claiming, and, of course, a complete clash of personalities happened more often than not. Thankfully, that hadn't been the case for Marc and Allie. Everything seemed to click from the moment they had met.

Marc pulled out to the tip and slammed back in, not knowing how much longer he could hold out.

"I want you to come with me," Allie begged.

"Are you sure about that, baby?" Gods, he wanted to come. Yet, part of him wanted to keep slamming in and out of her until he passed out from the sheer amount of pleasure ravaging his body.

"Yes! Fuck! Marc!" This time her voice was more of a demand than the begging she had done moments ago.

"Your wish is my command." He pumped his hips once more, feeling his seed climbing his cock. The pressure built until it finally burst, and his semen shot into her.

"Ohh!" she cried out, collapsing beneath him.

ELEVEN

ALLIE

Allie floated high in the clouds. It had become a serious problem keeping her ass grounded. It had been a week since she had met and mated Marc, and he was still all she could think about.

"Ms. Varga's in loooove," one of her middle schoolers sighed dreamily. A few others giggled, and several made gagging noises.

"I will neither confirm nor deny anything. Now, back to your tests." She winked at Lisa, the young girl who had called her daydreaming for exactly what it was. She and Marc had decided to keep their relationship between the two of them for now.

Allie had put off saying anything to her family

until she could tell them in person. She had dinner scheduled with them in T minus three hours. Just the thought of it alone made her stomach churn, and it shouldn't. She was happier than she had ever been and madly in love with her new mate. That was reason enough for her parents to be happy for her, but life was seldom that easy when it came to Alonzo Vasquez Varga and Maria Diego Varga.

Her parents may have looked like lovely people to strangers. They were well-to-do and lived in a prominent area. Her dad was the mayor of her hometown, which was right across the river from her house. Thankfully, in a different town, not under her dad's control.

Her friends had envied her growing up until they found out exactly what her parents were like and how demanding they truly were. Her life as a child and teen had not been easy. How could it have been when her mom had set the expectation that nothing short of perfection was acceptable, from her hair, to her clothes, to her grades?

None of it had been fun. The second Allie had the chance to flee she did, starting early in college and never looking back. Though her parents had paid her tuition and all expenses, she worked every minute she wasn't in class. The money she earned, she saved ... every penny of it ... knowing she'd need it after college.

"See you all on Monday," Allie said as the school day ended.

The last bell rang, announcing the end of Allie's day. Dread pooled in her stomach at the thought of seeing her parents. She had been over-the-moon happy ever since she had met Marc. Their relationship was one that she would describe as a whirlwind romance that had felt right in every way that mattered. There wasn't a single thing she would have done differently when it came to meeting and mating him.

So, what the hell was up with the dread that had started in her stomach and quickly spread to every limb of her body? The answer was as clear as the nose on her face. Allie was worried about her mother's reaction to her new mate. She knew the type of man her parents had expected her to marry. Marc did not fit into that 'top-of-his-class Harvard or Yale graduate' that her mother thought was best.

It was time to put on her big girl panties and face the music. No matter how much fuss her mom kicked up, Allie had to stand strong. It was her life to live, not her mother's. Marc was her fated mate.

Her mother had to see reason and accept it for what it was.

ALLIE TRIED NOT to sigh as her mother droned on and on about how proud she was of her cousin Caroline. She'd had a successfully arranged mating, and now the pair were getting married.

Yawn. Her beast thought, seriously unimpressed by the bullshit spewing from Maria's mouth.

"Allie, dear, have you thought any more about Clinton?" her mother asked.

"Clinton who?" Allie asked, setting her fork on her plate, knowing it would never be okay to keep eating while her mother talked directly to her.

Maria set her silverware down, crossed her hands over her lap, and squinted at Allie. It was a look she had seen many times and knew quite well. It was a look telling her that her mother was not amused and absolutely not fucking around. "Clinton Hollingsworth."

"Oh. Him. Mom, I'm really not interested in Clinton." Allie tried to sound neutral and completely unbiased, hoping her mother would drop the subject.

No such luck.

"Do you think you're too good for a man or mate like Clinton?" Her mother pressed on.

Allie knew her mother wasn't going to let it go. She sighed and tried to calm her nerves. Her fingers danced over the charmed necklace she wore around her neck. She'd had it spelled years ago to block her scent from all shifters. It had come in handy many times, and she knew it would get her in her parent's door without a single question. They knew she wore it to the human school she worked at to block her scent. That's why she was so surprised that Marc had scented her in the woods. But she firmly believed that being fated mates was the reason he could surpass the magic.

"Not at all, Mom. It's just that I met my mate already," she said. Her voice was nothing more than a whisper. She didn't dare meet the heavy stare of her mother or father.

"What's this?" her father set his silverware on his plate. She could feel the anger rolling off of him even though he sat on the opposite end of the ten-foot table.

Allie sucked in another deep breath and

decided to throw it out there for her parent to deal with. She gently unhooked her charmed necklace and slid it into her pocket.

"I said I've already met my mate." This time her voice was filled with pride. Gone was the worry about what they would think. She couldn't change how her parents acted, only how she reacted to them. She wasn't their little girl anymore. She'd been on her own as an adult for years.

"You let some random beast claim you?" her mother shouted.

"Mom, calm down. It's not like that. He isn't just some random beast I bumped into on the street. He's my mate, and yes, we've completed the mating ritual." Allie picked up her fork and took another bite of her dinner. If it was one thing she missed about living at home, it was Matthew's cooking. Matthew was the chef who had been with her family for as long as she could remember. The man was mad talented when it came to anything in the kitchen.

Allie spared a glance at her father and tried not to laugh. He looked as if he were readying to blow his top. Images of the old cartoons she used to watch flashed through her mind, and a small giggle escaped her mouth.

"You think this is funny? Are you ashamed to bring your new mate to meet your family? Are you ashamed of him?" her father asked.

"What! No! I'm not. He's a great man. He's kind and loving, and hardworking. I'm not embarrassed by him at all. I just wanted to tell you first that I'd found my mate, and you need to be nice to him." Allie shrugged.

"What do you mean by that?" her mom growled.

Another deep breath. "That you have a tendency to negatively overreact when things don't go as you hoped or planned." It wasn't a lie or an exaggeration. Allie had seen her mom flip her shit on way too many occasions. None of those occasions had ever been what she would call fun. Not in any way, shape, or form.

"I'll let that comment slide for now. Who is this man you've mated?" her mom asked.

"His name is Marcus Romero. Marc for short." Allie took another bite of her food. She felt her mom and dad's eyes on her and chose to ignore both of them.

"And?" her mother asked when she realized

Allie wasn't about to offer up any more information without being prompted to do so.

"And what? You asked for his name. I gave it to you." Allie bit her tongue, refusing to rise to her mother's bait. She would not get dragged into a huge blowout that would lead to her going low ... to no ... contact with them for the remainder of her natural life. It wasn't what she wanted. She wanted a normal, healthy relationship with the people who had given her life.

"And what exactly does Mr. Romero do for a living?" her dad asked.

"He's a firefighter in Rawley." Again, a simple and true answer with no elaboration.

"Jesus! Allie! What were you thinking? A firefighter? Really?" Her mom turned green. Straight up freaking green.

"Mom, stop. Just stop. You're not his mate. I am, and I love him." She placed her napkin over her plate and pushed it aside. So much for enjoying a fabulous dinner.

"You mate some riffraff, and I'm supposed to be perfectly okay with it. You might as well as have stepped in dog shit and tracked it all over the carpet."

"Are you kidding, Mom? All those years, you told me not to worry, that I'd find my mate someday. Was that just a bunch of bullshit, or what? Did you secretly hope and plot that I'd never find him? I swear, this family. I don't know why you can't just be happy for me." Allie was pissed. Not just regular pissed. She was super pissed. She was done being talked down to and made to feel like she wasn't worth the air she breathed.

"You think that we should be happy because you decided to mate with some lowlife?" her mom seethed, spittle flying from her mouth.

She'd never seen her mom so upset about anything. This definitely wasn't the reaction she had expected. Mad, yes. Crazy, a bit. Batshit crazy and in need of valium, no.

"He's not a lowlife. What is wrong with you? You act like he's some homeless man off the streets I just bumped into or something. He has a job. He has a home. He's a good man. Besides, he's my fated mate. If the fates thought he was good enough for me, you should too!" Allie shouted. "You know what? Never mind. It's not even worth wasting my breath on." Allie turned to leave. She didn't want to hear another fucking word out of her mom's mouth.

"Sit your ass down," her father shouted, stopping Allie in her tracks.

She wanted to move. She tried like hell to place one foot in front of the other and walk out the door, but she couldn't.

One glance around the room, and Allie knew why. His father's witch was present and keeping her trapped in an eerie mist that had suddenly filled the room.

"Let me go," she growled, her fangs pushing through her gums. Her beast wanted out to settle the score with the witch who was holding her captive against her will.

"I will do no such thing. You will sit and finish this conversation," her father said, never once leaving his seat. He had an uncanny ability to stay calm no matter what. The fact that he had shouted at her fell into the scary-as-hell category of behavior. He was the calm and collected type. Her mother was a force of nature who could never be calmed. It seems that finding out about her mating had flipped the script on her parents.

"We need to run," her tiger's voice filled her mind.

"I know, but the witch. We have nothing to

defend against her magic," Allie said, knowing she was well and truly fucked.

"How did you meet this mate of yours?"

Allie thought for a minute before she answered, hoping to come up with something that would calm her parents down. "I met with Gerri Wilder at the Paranormal Dating Agency." It was the absolute truth. Though, she did leave out the bit about meeting him on her camping trip and hitting it off from the minute they had met. And she certainly wasn't about to let them know they she couldn't keep her hands off him and jumped his bones within hours of meeting him.

Nope. Those were her thoughts and memories, and she was going to keep those bitches to herself.

"It's no wonder why you ended up mated to a loser. You went to a hack to find a mate."

"How dare you! You don't know a damn thing about my mate." A fire burned through Allie's veins. She was so tired of her parent's sanctimonious behavior. It wasn't even funny. She wasn't about to sit idly by while they disrespected a man they'd never once met.

"I know that he's not of a worthy station in life," her father said with an arched eyebrow. "That he doesn't have a degree from an Ivy League school. I know that no matter what, he will never be able to provide the type of home you are accustomed to."

"Type of home I'm accustomed to? What are you talking about?"

"Look around, Allie. Do you think we could have ever afforded such a lifestyle if we hadn't had a good education and a top-paying job?" her mother asked.

"This is your home. Not mine. My house is small and modest, and it's perfect for me. I don't need, nor do I want, all of this. It means nothing to me. You are obsessed with your lifestyle, not me. Or haven't you figured that out by now?"

"Don't speak to your mother like that," her dad barked at her.

"Look, I'm grateful for everything you did for me when I was younger, but I'm not you, Mom. I don't want the same things you do in life. I know how hard you've worked to have the perfect life. But that's not me. You have to know that by now. I love Marc, and he's my mate. That's the end of it. Now, let me go." She was done fighting, done explaining, and done with them.

"I'm sorry, honey. That's just not possible.

We'll fix this for you. Fix everything that you've messed up," her mom said.

"What! What are you talking about, Mom? Everything is ..."

The darkness started to seep in around Allie's vision. She fought like hell to push it back, but the witch's magic was just too damn strong. She had no idea what her parents were up to.

Panic ripped through her body, and her mind was going blank. Allie did the only thing she could do before she passed out. *"Marc! Help me! Please!"* she shouted, hoping her message would be carried through their mating connection.

TWELVE

MARC

Marc flipped through the channels, trying to find something to entertain him until Allie showed up. He didn't know why but he'd been restless all damn day, knowing that she was going to meet her parents and tell them about their mating. She'd seemed nervous the night before about talking to them, and that didn't sit well with him at all. He wondered for the hundredth time why she would be nervous about telling them that she had met her mate.

He had stopped by his mom's home on his way home from Allie's house the first day they had been back from the impromptu camping trip to let her know that he had found and claimed his mate. His mom had been ecstatic ... so had his siblings. It was a joyous occasion to be celebrated.

Hell, his sisters had gone with him to help him pick out the engagement ring. He pulled the box from his pocket and flipped the lid open. Staring at the three-carat diamond surrounded by a dozen tiny diamonds, he couldn't help the smile that spread across his face.

Marc wanted Allie in his arms, kissing him as she said yes to his proposal. Though they were already mated, he wanted it to be official in all ways. Both in the shifter world and in the human world. He wanted Allie in ways he had never wanted another.

He tucked the ring back into the box and slid it into his pocket for safekeeping. Then he continued flipping through the channels until he found a high-octane action flick, hoping it would occupy his mind for a few hours.

Deciding that no matter what movie or TV show he put on was pretty damn useless, he clicked the TV off and shot off a quick text to Allie.

Heading to my mom's for a bit. Text me when you are on your way. Good luck with your parental units.

Days off for Marc were hell. He never quite

knew what to do with himself. He usually volunteered to work, or he'd help his mom with projects around her house. Since all the shifts were covered at the station, he headed to his mom's to work on the ongoing list of repairs to her older home.

The short drive took less than ten minutes before he found himself sitting in the driveway.

"What are you doing just sitting there looking like you're lost, baby boy?" his mom, Judith, asked, knocking on his truck window.

"Hey, Mom. Sorry. I guess I don't know. I feel off. Like anxious. It's weird." He tried to explain the nagging feeling in his gut, but it was hard to explain when he couldn't exactly pinpoint the issue.

She pressed the back of her hand over his forehead. "You're not running a fever."

"Such a mom thing to do." Marc laughed, leaning down to give her a hug. "I said I felt off, not sick."

"Where's Allie tonight? Are we still on for Sunday dinner so we can finally meet her?"

"She's telling her parents about us tonight. She was really nervous about it, but I don't understand why. And yes, we're still on for Sunday. She's looking forward to it." A wave of nausea hit him hard. He felt his stomach churn. The anxiety he'd been feeling turned into sheer panic and almost brought him to his knees.

"Marc!" his mom yelled. "Are you okay?"

"Something's wrong," he shouted, feeling like his heart was going to explode.

"Marc! Help me! Please!" he heard Allie's voice in his head, calling out for help. His beast charged forward, demanding control of their body. He felt his fangs punch through his gums, his eyes stinging as his face started to transform into that of his tiger.

"Easy, Marc. Talk to me. Tell me what's wrong," his mom begged. Her calming voice broke through the overwhelming emotions wreaking havoc on his body.

"It's Allie! There's something wrong with her. I heard her in my head screaming for help. How is this even possible," he said, still fighting the urge to shift.

"Calm yourself. You must remain in control of your form. You won't be any good to Allie if you turn into a senseless beast hell-bent on revenge." She ran her fingers lightly up and down his arm calming him as only a mother could.

"I know, but ..."

"Where do her parents live?" she asked.

"I don't know. She didn't say." Marc pulled his phone from his pocket and hit the speed dial for Gerri Wilder.

"Good idea," his mom said as he pushed the speaker button on his phone.

"Marc. How are you? I'm assuming all has gone well with your mating," Gerri said as she answered his call.

"There's something wrong with Allie, and I don't know how to find her," Marc yelled into the phone.

"What's the matter? What's happened?" Gerri asked. He could hear the panic in her voice.

"She called out for help through our mating connection. She was going to tell her parents about our mating today. Something's wrong with her. I can't ... I can't feel her anymore."

"Oh shit! Gimme a second."

He heard Gerri's fingers fly across her keyboard.

"Fuck! Fuck! Why didn't I realize this before?" she shouted.

"What is it? What did you find?" he asked, quickly losing what little patience he had left. With his tiger demanding he find their mate and his own anxiety over the situation, Marc didn't know how much longer he could hold his shit together.

"Her parents are part of a fanatical group. A group that still practices arranged marriages based on family, social connections, and money."

"So they basically sell off their daughters to the highest bidder?" Judith spat.

"Exactly," Gerri confirmed his mom's suspicion.

"Who are they, and where do they live? I don't care what I have to do. I will save Allie from those sick fuckers if it's the last thing I do," Marc growled.

"And what are you going to do? Run in there half-cocked? Are you trying to get yourself killed?" Judith shouted at her son.

"Mom, what do you expect me to do? I can't just sit here, knowing Allie is in trouble, and do nothing. I have to help her. I have to save her. Every instinct in my body is telling me to act. To do something. Anything. Even if it means giving my life so she may live. You know how the mating connection works. I can't fight it."

He was going fucking crazy. Beating back his tiger took more brain power and physical strength than he currently had. His everything was quickly waning.

"I'm on my way. Don't do anything until I get there." Gerri ended the call and left Marc staring down at his phone.

"What the hell is she supposed to do? How is she going to take on her parents, who are both tigers? And who the hell else knows who's there with them?" Marc asked.

"I'm sure she'll come up with something. Let me call your brothers and get them here. You can't do this alone. I won't lose you to these sadistic people."

Marc nodded. Not knowing what else to say. His mom was right. He had no idea what the hell he would be running into. Allie was a strong woman and even stronger in her animal form. He had to believe that her parents wouldn't actually hurt her. They must've had some sort of a plan to get her away from him. He'd have to be calm, even if it was just for a little bit.

He took a deep breath, then another, hoping it would help to soothe his mind and clear his head.

It didn't.

His mom's hurried words to his brothers reached his ears, and he tried to fight off another wave of panic. He unlocked his phone and began to google his mate, hoping to find anything he could ... most importantly, who her family was and any address that might be listed for them.

After scrolling for a few minutes, he came across a picture of her with her family and recognized the faces of her parents immediately.

"Son of a bitch!" he shouted.

"What's wrong?" Judith asked. "What's the matter? What did you find?" She quickly cut off her call and closed the distance between them.

"Look. That's Allie with her parents." He held up his phone to show his mom the picture he'd found online.

"It looks like he has power and prestige far beyond our means. Now what?" she asked.

"I have no idea. Hopefully, Gerri has some ideas on how the hell we are supposed to do this."

"Oh, baby boy. I don't even know what to say other than this isn't good."

"Nope. Not at all." Marc closed the screen on his phone and tucked it into his pocket. He had to find a way to save his mate ... no matter what. Even if her dad was the damn mayor.

THIRTEEN

ALLIE

Allie's eyes slowly blinked open. Her mouth felt as if it had been stuffed full of cotton balls, and her head pounded. She quickly closed her eyes again, hoping the pain would go away, but continued to nag at her. Opening her eyes again, she sucked in a deep breath, feeling like she had been drugged.

That's when it all came back to her in a flash. She'd been having dinner with her parents, telling them about her mating with Marc.

"Oh, no!" she whispered and sat straight up on the bed, finding herself in her childhood bedroom. No wonder she felt like she had been drugged. It was magic from her father's witch that was keeping her mind foggy. She tried to shake it off, but it clung to her like bad perfume, and it smelled just as bad.

"I hate fucking witches!" she growled through the pain.

"Awe, honey. You shouldn't say things like that. You'll end up with a nasty hex if you keep the shit up," the witch in question said.

Allie hadn't seen her sitting on the chair in the corner.

"Why are you doing this?" she asked the woman.

"Because your daddy pays well. Why else?" she said with a smile.

Allie wanted to knock that smile right off her beautiful face. Even sitting, she could tell the blonde had legs that went on for days. They probably had their own damn zip code. Her hair was short and looked as if it had been cut by a weed whacker. Even that didn't take away a single bit of her unnatural beauty. Her full lips had been painted bright red and clashed with her dark purple eyes. Yet, she was still the most beautiful woman Allie had ever laid her eyes on.

"Easy, honey. Or I'm going to start thinking you like me more than that mutt of a mate you claim to be in love with," the witch snarked. An evil smile spread across her face. It was then that Allie noticed the witch's teeth had been filed into points and tipped with silver.

"Uh, hardly. I'm trying to figure out what it is about you. What seems so off. Other than the fact that you're a witch," Allie said, trying to put her finger on what was drawing her to the woman.

"I'm just that hot. Try not to overthink it, honey. I wouldn't want you to hurt that pretty little head of yours."

Allie rolled her eyes. "You really are a piece of work, aren't you?" She eyed her up and down once again and saw the witch's magic flicker. Allie kept her mouth shut, not wanting the witch to know that she had caught that. The witch wasn't who she looked like at all. Her looks came from a spell.

She should have known there was nothing natural about the way she looked. The witch wasn't some young, hot, powerful woman. The spell that she had cast over her much older and heavier body was starting to fade, drawing much more power than she had considered.

"How long do you plan on keeping me here?" Allie asked, wanting to force the witch to keep up her illusion spell. The longer she kept her occupied, the more magic it would require.

"Until your parents do what needs to be done." The witch shrugged.

"And what exactly is that?" Allie asked, wanting to know what her parents had in store for her.

"Wouldn't you like to know?" the witch teased.

"Actually, I would. Because whatever it is, it needs to be stopped. I've found my mate, and that is the end of the story." Allie couldn't believe how her parents had reacted. Actually, she could. She'd just hoped things would have turned out differently. Hoped her parents would have acted differently and accepted her mating.

"Too bad. So sad. You'll find out soon enough. I have to admit, though, I'm surprised by the vindictiveness of a mother and father toward their daughter. I'm a witch, and even I think it's cold as fuck. Guess you should have listened to them, and you wouldn't be in this mess."

"Mess? That's what you want to call being held hostage?" Allie asked.

"Pretty much. Feel free to pick another term if you'd like. I don't really give a fuck either way. As I said, the only reason I'm here is for the money."

"It must suck to be you," Allie said. She needed to find a way to wear the witch down. If she could get her to use up her already failing magic, she could put an end to this and get the fuck out of there before her parents even realized she was gone.

"It's like I can see the hamster running and the wheel turning in your head, trying to come up with some sort of plan to make your great escape. It won't work. So don't even bother trying, honey."

"I don't know what you're talking about." Allie would deny, deny, deny. She would not give her captor anything that would be useful against her.

"Uh-huh. Sure."

"Why don't you fetch my parents so we can get this shit over with. I've got plans today. Besides, I'm bored." Allie knew she needed to piss the witch off, even if it hurt just a bit to do it.

"Allie, can you hear me?" Marc's voice filled her mind. Her tiger pushed forward, wanting her mate, but Allie pushed her back, knowing that shifting into a giant tiger at that moment would not be helpful. Not only that, but she'd also likely end up on the wrong side of a witch's wand.

"Marc! Marc! Oh! Thank God! My parents have lost their minds." She had never been so damn happy in her life to hear his voice in her head.

"Are you okay, baby? Please tell me they didn't

hurt you. I was so worried when you just disappeared, and I couldn't reach you."

"No. They didn't hurt me. They had their witch knock me out. She's holding me hostage in my old bedroom, but her magic is waning. I can see that her illusion spell is starting to fade. I don't think she realizes how much of her energy she's using to keep up her ruse."

"What do you think I am? Your dog? I don't fucking think so," the witch snarled at her.

Allie stood, getting more pissed off by the second. "Look, you can either get my parents, or you can take me to them. I'm done fucking around with all of you." If she could push the witch just a little harder and sap the rest of her magic, she'd be home free with no one the wiser to her plans.

"Sit down and shut up before I make you take another nap, honey. You don't want to get on my bad side," the witch said.

"You mean you have a good side?" Allie snarked.

The witch stood and closed the distance between her and Allie. "I've been nice so far. Don't make me hurt you because I will."

"Ohhh. I'm so scared," Allie teased.

The witch's magic flickered. "I'm not kidding.

This is your final warning. Sit down and shut up before I sit you down and shut you up."

"Please. What the fuck are you going to do? You realize I'm a full-grown tiger, right?"

"And I'm a full-grown witch. I'll have no problem dropping your ass like I did earlier." The witch pulled her wand from her pocket and aimed it directly at Allie's head.

"Fine, go for it. Do you think you can take me out? But just know now that you better hope like fuck that you can run faster than me in tiger form if you miss because I will kill you," Allie growled. She flashed her fangs, proving she wasn't fucking around.

The witch flicked her wrist, and a flash of energy shot out at Allie, which she quickly sidestepped, dodging the deadly magic. The witch followed up with another blast of magic, and once again, Allie was easily slid out of the way. The blasts of magic landed against the wall, leaving large, charred circles on the wallpaper.

"Your aim sucks." Allie laughed, taunting the witch. Allie bit back a smile as the witch's magic flickered again. Her plan was working.

"You little bitch!" she screeched and fired off two more bolts of magic in rapid succession.

Allie dodged the first, but the witch had anticipated her moves this time, and the second bolt grazed her right shoulder, causing her to wince in pain. The pain pissed her off even more than she had already been. She was done with the situation. She was done with being held against her will and absolutely done with her parents trying to force their choices on her life.

"Is that all you got?" Allie seethed at the woman.

"Just a little longer," she told her tiger. *"Be ready. She's about to use up the rest of her magic. Then that bitch is ours."*

The sooner, the better, her animal replied.

"Your parents are going to be pissed when they come home and find you dead, but I don't even care at this point. They paid in advance." The witch raised her wand again and pointed it directly at Allie's heart.

"It's now or never," Allie told her tiger.

I'm ready!

She saw the witch's magic flicker once again, and that's when Allie struck. She willed her beast forward, but only barely, just enough to turn her fingers into claws. Feeling the snap of the bones in her hands, she smiled at the witch.

"Yes. They will be pissed when they come home and find you dead."

She struck the witch quickly and hard, slashing her carotid wide open. Blood splattered against her bright pink bedroom walls, making it look like a scene from a horror movie.

By the time the witch knew what was about to happen, she was already on the floor, gagging on her own blood.

Allie didn't feel a single ounce of remorse. Why should she when the woman her parents had hired had been nothing short of evil and sadistic?

FOURTEEN

MARC

Marc felt a sharp pain slice through his arm. His heart hammered. At first, he thought it was fear that was causing his heart to pound, but it wasn't. It was pure adrenaline. He quickly realized that it wasn't his pain or adrenaline but that of his mate.

"Allie, baby. Are you okay? What happened?" he asked her through the mating connection.

"I'm fine. The witch is dead. I'm leaving now. I'll let you know as soon as I'm in my car, and this place is in my rearview mirror."

"Marc, is Allie okay?" his mom asked just as Gerri pulled into the driveway.

"Yeah. She said the witch is dead, and she's trying to make her escape now."

"Good!" Gerri said, stepping toward the group that had assembled.

Marc, his mom, and all of his siblings stood on the front porch waiting for Gerri to arrive.

"Yes. Very good," Marc said as Gerri pulled him into a tight hug.

"I don't think we should wait to find out what happens. I think we need to go now," Judith said. "None of this sits right with me. What kind of parent treats their child like a piece of property instead of a living being?"

Marc had only ever seen his mom this angry once before. He knew the string that was holding her together was near snapping. He was surprised it hadn't already. Even though she had yet to meet Allie, she still considered her one of her children. And no one fucked with her family ... ever.

"I think your mom is right, Marc. These people are ... demented. I hate to say that about someone, but it's true. I will never understand these fundamentalists," Gerri said. "We should go now in case Allie needs help. I'm glad to see you've recruited the family to help. We're likely going to need everyone's strength. The witch may be out of play, but we have no idea who else is involved in their sick scheme."

"She's right," Marc said. "Split up into two vehicles. We'll park a block away. I'll take group one around to the front of the house for the straight-on confrontation. Group two will circle around the back of the property and only help if needed. Mom and Gerri are with me. Ryan, you take Ben and Ella with you, and do not let them get hurt."

"Please. We know how to take care of ourselves." Ella punched him playfully in the side. "Let a bitch come at me, and I'll bite her fucking head off."

"I know you will, sis. Just be safe. You've been kickin' ass and takin' names since you were in diapers."

Yeah, Ella knew how to take care of herself, but Marc still worried about his baby sister. He would kill anyone who hurt her ... zero fucking questions asked.

Once they had broken into their groups, they set off on their mission of finding Marc's mate.

"Allie, can you hear me? We're on our way."

"Marc! Oh, God! They have me. They've lost their damn minds! You have to stay away. It's not safe. They'll kill you! Please! Do not come here. I'll figure out a way out of this mess!"

"Fuck!" Marc punched his steering wheel and immediately regretted the action the second his airbag deployed. He quickly veered toward the curb and came to a quick stop.

"Honey, what happened?" Judith asked.

Marc and Gerri jumped out of the truck. "Her parents have her," he said, kicking the tire of his truck. "She said not to come. That she would figure it out. That her parents would kill me. I can't just do nothing."

"And we won't. There are enough of us to take on anyone they throw at us. We can do this. We will save Allie," Judith placed a comforting hand on his shoulder.

"We need to get there now," Gerri said.

Marc glanced up at the darkening sky and cursed again. "Fuck! I agree. Who knows what is going on over there? I need her in my arms and safe ... now."

"We will get there faster on four legs as opposed to two," Judith said, stating the obvious now that Marc's truck was out of commission thanks to his temper getting the best of him.

"Thankfully, it's dark out now, and the streets are pretty quiet. Try to keep to the tree line and out of sight of people. The last thing we need is to have animal control called for someone seeing two tigers and a wolf running through town," Gerri said.

"If we're going to do this, let's do it," Marc said. He felt the magic in the air around him thicken as Gerri shifted to her wolf form, and his mom shifted into her tiger form and let out a low grumble.

Marc sucked in a deep breath and let the control go to his animal. His transformation was happening faster than it ever had. When he glanced toward the ground, he stood on four legs instead of two. He didn't waste a second. Feeling his powerful muscles spring into action, he headed for Allie's parents' house.

His muscles burned as he raced at a breakneck speed to reach his mate.

"Allie, where are you? Talk to me, baby. What is going on?" he asked, needing to know what the hell was happening with her parents.

"Marc! They are trying to find a way to break my mating bond with you! They have another witch here, and she's getting ready to do some sort of spell! Please! Oh, God!"

Anger tore through him. He could hear the fear in her voice, and it broke his heart. Whatever the hell her parents were up to had to be stopped. She was his fated mate, and he would not let anyone come between them. It didn't matter who the fuck they were. No one would tear him from his mate. Not when he'd just found her after spending his whole life dreaming about her and searching for her.

"Hang on, baby! We'll be there soon."

FIFTEEN

ALLIE

"Why are you doing this?" Allie shouted at her mom and dad. She was reaching the point of having a full-blown panic attack. She had been home free after she had killed the witch. After all, the witch had said that her parents were gone. Allie had almost made it. If she would have only jumped out of her bedroom window rather than running down the stairs and through the front door, she would have been free of the people who had raised her and now were hell-bent on destroying her.

"Because we know what is best for you, and being mated to a piece of trash is not the path we will allow you to go down. It's a shame you had to go and kill the other witch, but Helena won't make the same mistakes. She is much more powerful than you can imagine, and she won't fall for your tricks," her father said.

"I don't know what you are planning, but my mate has already claimed me, and I've claimed him. You can't keep us apart! Not when the fates have decreed it."

"That's what Helena is for. She can easily break a mating bond and erase that piece of trash from your memory," her mother growled.

"Mom! You can't do this. I love him. I want to spend the rest of my life with him." For the first time in her life, Allie truly feared her parents. They had gone off the deep end. There were no ands, ifs, or buts about it. They had sunken to a whole new level of low that Allie had hoped to never witness. Not only had they threatened to break her mating bond, but they also threatened to take her memories of Marc.

Just when she thought it couldn't get any worse, Clinton Hollingsworth stepped into the room. "Clinton! What are you doing here?"

"Allie." His smile was genuine. He'd always seemed like such a sweet guy, but there had never been a spark between them. Not even a tiny one.

"I've tried to woo you. I've tried to get you to agree to be mine. You are the one for me, Allie. You always have been." His voice was soft and soothing like always, but his look was one of sheer menace.

"No! Clinton, you're a nice guy. Do not let them drag you into this. I've found my mate. My fated mate and we've claimed each other. Please don't do this. Please!" she begged.

He ran the back of his hand down her cheek softly before wrapping his fingers tightly around her throat. "You will be fine. Helena will make sure of it. As soon as your bond is broken with the trash you think is your mate, I will make you my mate, and we will be together forever."

If her arms weren't chained to the chair, she would have ripped his damn throat out. He was no better than her parents. "I should have known you were a piece of shit. So help me, God, when I get out of these chains, I will kill you."

"So much sass. It will be fun to bend you to my will," he growled, his eyes flashing.

Alonzo nodded to Helena. "We need to get this over with before that beast of hers shows up. She's probably been talking to him through their mating connection the whole time."

"I'm surprised he hasn't broken down the door

already," Helena said and closed the distance between her and Allie. "Sorry, child, but this will hurt." She placed her hands on each of Allie's temples and began to chant in some strange language.

Pain shot through her head and quickly consumed her entire body. She let out a horrifying scream as the witch's chants grew louder and louder. Allie's head felt like it was going to explode from the pain.

Images of her first meeting Marc flashed through her mind and slowly disappeared. As soon as one image vanished, another of her time with him popped into her head, then disappeared just as quickly. She could feel her memories of him fading. Seconds later, she saw them in bed together. Saw the moment she turned her head and submitted to Marc's bite. It was the single best moment of her life, and like the others, it quickly disappeared into oblivion.

"Stop! Stop! Don't do this, please!" she shouted, but the witch kept chanting, never slowing the words spewing from her mouth. Allie fought back, trying to push the witch out of her mind, but nothing seemed to work. She rocked back and forth, trying to break the chains or the chair she had been strapped to. It didn't matter to her which broke first so long as one of them did. She couldn't let the witch finish her spell. Couldn't let her break her connection with Marc or the love she had for him.

"Hold her still," her father shouted.

Clinton came around behind her and placed his hands on her shoulders. "I've got her. She's not going anywhere. Finish this, now."

"No! Let me go," Allie cried out again. An image flipped into her mind. This time it was her fangs sinking into Marc's neck. She tried to hold onto the memory, but the witch yanked the thought right out of her brain. Her chest warmed. It felt like a flame had been lit and was being sucked from her body. She felt it travel from her heart to her mind.

"No! No! No!" she cried to her tiger, who fought the magic just as hard as she did.

The witch suddenly stopped chanting. The room went quiet. The thick magic surrounding Allie subsided, and she tried to remember what she was so damn upset about.

"What happened?" she asked her parents, who stood nearby, looking concerned for her.

"Allie! Oh, Allie! Are you okay?" her mom ran to her side.

"Yeah, I'm fine. What is going on? Why am I chained to this chair? Dad, please say something."

"It is done," Helena said and took a step back.

"What's done? Why are you all looking at me like that?" Allie couldn't figure out what the hell was going on and why her parents were acting so strange.

Her father finally stepped forward and unlocked the chains holding her in place. "We were worried that someone had placed a spell on you to hurt you, but Helena assures me that there's nothing to worry about, sweetheart. You're all good." He pulled her into a hug.

"Oh, thank God! But who would have done such a thing?" she asked. "Who would target me and why?"

"You know I have a difficult campaign coming up, dear. I'm afraid that one of my opponents is up to no good and hoped to get to you in order to destroy our family."

"What! Are you serious? How is that even allowed? Aren't there laws against that?" she asked. Though her father had brought up the possibility of things like this happening when she was younger, she figured that as an adult, she would be in the clear when it came to being a liability for her father's political career.

"There are laws against it and don't worry, dear, we are working with the police department. But we wanted to make sure that no one had compromised you," her father said.

"Thanks, Daddy." Allie wrapped her arms around her father and returned his hug.

"I will always protect you, no matter what the threat is," Alonzo said.

Allie knew in her heart that her dad would always protect her, even with their rocky past, even if they hadn't always seen eye to eye on everything. She pulled back from the hug and rubbed her wrists.

"Clinton, what are you doing here?" Allie asked.

"I asked him over for dinner tonight, sweetie." Her mom smiled at her.

"Oh. That's nice. How's your mom?" she turned to Clinton and asked.

"She's great, as always. She wanted me to tell you to stop by sometime. She said it's been a while since she's seen you."

"It has been. I'll have to set something up to

pop in one day after work." It had been months since she'd seen Mrs. Hollingsworth. She used to stop in and have tea with her regularly, but ever since her husband had passed, Mrs. Hollingsworth had stopped seeing visitors during her time of mourning. Not that Allie could blame her. If she'd lost the mate she had spent the last fifty years with, she imagined her mourning would be profound as well.

There was a bang at the front door, pulling Allie from her thoughts. "Did you invite someone else?" she asked.

"No. Why don't you let Clinton escort you to the dining room while I see who it is? I'll just be a minute."

Allie nodded, but something felt off. *"It's probably just the witch's magic,"* she said to her tiger, thinking that must have been what was affecting her.

I don't know. There's something strange about this whole situation, her tiger replied.

Allie shrugged it off, not knowing what to make of it, and turned to face Clinton. He held his arm out for her. "Always the perfect gentleman," she said, smiling up at him.

SIXTEEN

MARC

He'd tried to contact her through their mating connection several times, but she failed to answer. Just as he rounded the block to her parent's house, it felt like his soul had been ripped right from his body. He stumbled and instantly shifted back to his human form.

"Marc! What's wrong?" His mom quickly shifted to her human form and helped him up off the ground.

"Allie! I can't feel her anymore. It's like my connection to her dissolved. Like she's not even there. Like our mating connection is gone."

"The witch. It has to be," Gerri said, quickly shifting to her human form as well.

Marc stood, hanging his head toward the ground. It felt as if his heart had been ripped from his chest. Whatever he and Allie had shared was gone. He felt it. His wolf felt it. And it fucking sucked. The woman he loved, and he had mated ... their connection had been erased as if it had never existed to begin with.

"The house is just on the other side of the trees," Gerri said. "We have to ..."

"Have to what? It's done. I'm too late." Marc felt like what remained of his heart was breaking into a million pieces.

"Listen to me, Marc. Allie is still your mate. Even if the connection has been broken by a witch, it can be re-established," Gerri said. "Just because they want to keep the two of you apart doesn't mean the fates will allow this foolishness to stand. Everyone knows you can't fight fate. Now, pull up your big boy panties and quit pouting. You've got a mate that needs saving."

At that moment, something in his brain clicked. Gerri was right. He heard the truth in her words and felt that same truth even deeper in his bones. His tiger rallied inside his mind.

She is still our mate. Even if she no longer knows it, his tiger growled.

He closed his eyes and replayed his memories of them together. The first time he saw her, scented her. The smile on her face as they kissed for the first time. The way she shivered every time he touched her. The way it felt when he was buried balls deep inside her. How much he loved her. He would not let anyone take that away from them. He would fight for her.

With his mind made up, he sprinted the last few yards to her house and banged on the ornate door. Even through the brick of the house and the heavy wooden barrier, he could smell his mate. She was still there.

Seconds passed, and no one answered. He pounded his fist against the door again, ready to kick the fucking thing in if no one answered soon. He didn't give a shit if it was the mayor's house or not.

The deadbolt released, and the door creaked open. He was greeted by none other than the mayor himself. The sly grin on his face told Marc all he needed to know. The mayor had been expecting him, and he was too late. He wanted nothing more than to wipe that fucking grin off his damn face.

"Where is she? Where's my mate?" Marc

shouted the second the front door opened. He knew she was inside; he could smell her scent everywhere. Gerri and his mom flanked him on either side.

"I don't know what you're talking about or who you are. I suggest you leave before I have you removed," the man said.

"Where is she?" Fury pounded through Marc. "I'm not leaving without my mate." His fangs punched through his gums. It took every ounce of his willpower to stay in human form and not rip this fucker's head right off his shoulders.

The man's eyes flashed. A clear warning to him. "I suggest you back the fuck up, son. As I said, you have no business here. Now, leave."

"I can smell her ... everywhere. Allie! Allie! Where are you?" Marc shouted, pushing his way past her dad and into the foyer.

Alonzo grabbed him by the shoulder, trying to push him back toward the door. "Get the hell out before I call the police."

"You can try to hide behind the law all you want, Mayor, but we both know this isn't something that will be handled by the police. Allie!" Marc shouted again, his mom and Gerri barging in behind him.

"Let go of me! Who's there? Who is that?" Allie shouted, pushing her way past Clinton.

"It's no one, love. Let your dad handle it," Clinton said, trying to pull her back toward the dining room.

"Allie!" Marc shouted. "Get your hands off of my mate!" Marc was seconds away from snapping and releasing his tiger. He'd let his beast figure this shit out.

"Mate? Who are you?" Allie asked.

It broke his heart even more to see the look of confusion on her face. She truly had no idea who the hell he was.

"I will kill you for this. And the witch you used to erase her memories of me. Do you understand me?" Marc charged Alonzo. He didn't care if Allie was standing right there. He would end her father for what he had done to break their mating. In the shifter world, that was grounds for death. Packs had fought all-out wars over such infractions. Everyone knew that you simply did not fuck with one's mate.

Period.

"Easy, Marc," Gerri said. "I'm sure we can figure this out with the mayor."

"And you are?" Alonzo asked.

"Gerri Wilder."

"And what do you have to do with this, Ms. Wilder?" he sneered at her. The look on his face was one generally reserved for when you stepped in dog shit.

"Gerri, what are you doing here?" Allie asked, looking even more confused.

"You know her?" her mother asked, glancing toward Helena, who held up her hands and offered a slight shrug.

"You didn't say anything about her," Helena said.

"What do you mean by that?" Allie asked Helena.

The witch walked away and went to stand by Maria.

"Allie, can we please just talk?" Marc asked. If he could just talk to her, he could explain everything. He didn't know how to prove to her that he was, indeed, her mate, but he had to try.

SEVENTEEN

ALLIE

"Dad, what is he talking about? Who is this?" Allie had no idea who the sexy stranger was, but damn ... her hormones went wild the second he barged his way into her parents' house, spouting something about them being mates.

"I don't know who he is or what he wants," Alonzo said, never taking his eyes off Marc.

She could hear the lie in her father's voice. So did her tiger.

"Something is up, but I don't know what it is. Do you have any idea?" she asked her animal.

I have no idea what the hell is going on other than the fact that he is MINE!

It took all the strength Allie had not to shift right there and rub up against the sexy stranger, but she held her ground, not wanting to stir up any more ruckus.

"Who are you? How do you know me?" she tried to step closer to Marc, but Clinton pulled her back. "Let go, Clinton. I'm fine. I don't know how, but I know he won't hurt me."

"No, I can't allow it," Clinton growled.

"Excuse me?" Allie turned to face Clinton. The look on his face suddenly changed from the caring, sweet man she knew to someone altogether different. Anger rolled off him in waves. His scent seemed wrong. She had always felt safe around Clinton until now.

Before Allie could even bat so much as an eyelash, Clinton tossed her over her shoulder and headed for the kitchen.

"Put me down, you asshole!" She punched at his back and kicked at his chest, trying to get him to loosen his grip around her waist, but it was useless. He had her in a tight hold and was not letting go.

"Allie!" the man named Marc shouted again. She lifted herself up to see the look on his face. It haunted her. Whoever he was, mate or not, he clearly cared for her, and it was evident by the events taking place. She punched at Clinton's back again. Still, he refused to let go.

I can make him let go, her tiger offered.

"Do it. Do it now!" Allie said. *"I don't know what is going on here, but something isn't right."*

Agreed.

Allie allowed her beast to take over without giving it a second thought. Her fangs elongated, and her hand shifted into a paw. While swiping at Clinton's back, she buried her fangs into his shoulder and bit down as hard as she could.

"Ouch! What the fuck!" Clinton shouted, tossing her to the ground.

Allie quickly continued her shift as Clinton drew his booted foot up to her face. She swiped at his leg, drawing blood across his upper thigh.

"Stop!" Alonzo shouted just as Clinton started to shift. "We only want what's best for you."

And didn't that statement from her father just piss her off? Allie let out a loud growl, warning them to stay away from her. She needed time to think. To clear her head and figure out what the hell was going on.

Rushing through the kitchen, she barreled

through the back door, knocking three people she'd never met onto their asses. She didn't have time to care or even to look back. Her instinct was telling her to get the fuck out of there, and for once, she was going to listen.

Her legs burned from the exertion. Allie didn't think she'd ever run so hard and fast in her entire life. Staying at her parent's home to figure things out simply wasn't an option. Not when she knew that her father was lying through his teeth.

She should have known that something was up. She tried to play nice when it came to being chained to a freaking chair. But that ended the second Clinton had tossed her over his shoulder and tried to get her away from the stranger claiming to be her mate. None of it made a freaking lick of sense. Allie had so many questions that she didn't even know where to start.

Why didn't she remember the events up to that moment? If they had simply been looking for proof that someone had tried to compromise her, why couldn't she remember anything before that moment at her parent's house? Allie thought back, racking her brain about the last thing she remembered.

"I dismissed the kids for the day and gathered my things. From there, I got into my car and headed to my parents. The very next memory was of Helena standing in front of me. Then, I was chained to the chair, wondering what the fuck was going on. Something is missing," she said to her tiger.

That's an understatement!

Allie heard several branches snapping behind her. The sounds of low moans and chuffs sounded behind her. She picked up her speed, not wanting to have to deal with Clinton or her parents again. Sticking to the trees, Allie raced to the far edges of town and crossed through the winding creek toward her house.

The footfalls behind her picked up as she neared her house. Her heart raced, worried that Clinton would try to pull more shit with her and carry her off to wherever he had planned before she had ruined it for him.

Nope. She wasn't doing that shit again. She may be a full-grown female tiger, but he was a male of the same species. Allie might be able to get in a few good hits, but his size alone gave him the advantage. And he could take her down easier than she cared to admit.

Just as she approached the last stretch to her house, her animal slammed on the brakes and spun around to face the approaching threat.

"What! What are you doing? Why did you stop?" she chided her tiger.

Trust me. He won't hurt us!

"He who?" Allie asked. "We need to keep running! We need to get as far away from all of this as possible." Allie pleaded with her tiger to see sense, but it refused to budge from their spot.

Within seconds, a male tiger raced toward her. He skidded to a stop in front of her. It was the sexy stranger from her parent's house. His cinnamon and wild-man scent rushed over her, leaving her staggering. God, he smelled so fucking good. She wanted nothing more than to forget everything that had happened tonight and rub against him.

There was something familiar about those striking green eyes of his. It was almost as if she knew him from somewhere, though she couldn't quite put her finger on where. He shifted to his human form, causing her to suck in a sharp breath. Damn, he was stunning as an animal and as a human.

"It would be easier to talk to you if you would shift," he said.

His voice was music to her ears. She thought about his request for a few seconds before complying and shifting into her human form. Allie had questions. Hopefully, he had the answers she needed.

EIGHTEEN

MARC

Marc had never been so happy to see his mate. After her bold move of taking down the shifter she called Clinton, he flew out the front door, anticipating her move. He yelled for his mom and Gerri to head home while he chased down Allie.

At first, he'd been worried about leaving them alone at the house of torture, but they had assured him they would be just fine. His mom told him that she'd kick his ass if he didn't go after his mate. Marc didn't need any further encouragement. He took off after her faster than a jackrabbit on the run from a pack of hungry wolves.

He needed to talk to her. To figure out how to fix things. To fix what had been taken from them and to convince her that she was his mate. He would never forgive her parents for their interference in their relationship. And if he ever got his paws on that fucking witch, Helena, she'd lose her damn head. He swore to the gods.

"Fine. I'm in human form. Who are you, and what do you have to do with all of this?"

He breathed a sigh of relief that she had stopped running and decided to talk to him.

"I'm Marc Romero."

"What do you want? How do you know my parents?" she asked.

Her guard was up. He understood that. After all she'd been through, he would have been surprised if she was relaxed and calm.

"I don't know your parents. I've never met them before. I came to the house because you're my mate. You were supposed to tell your parents tonight about our mating. You've been nervous about it all week but wouldn't tell me why. I thought it was odd, but I wanted to give you space when it came to your relationship with your parents," he said, hoping that something in her memory sparked.

"How do you know Gerri Wilder?" Allie asked, ignoring his other questions.

"I went to her to find my mate. She told me about your camping trip last week. I met you up there, and one thing led to another." God, his memories of their first encounter would be forever engrained into his brain.

"Oh, God! We slept together!" Allie sucked in a deep breath. A blush covered her cheeks and heated her neck.

Fuck, she was beautiful when she was all flustered.

"We did much more than that," he said, closing the distance between them. "You have to feel this connection we have. Allie, whatever you think right now, listen to your instincts. We are mates. You can feel the truth in your veins. You know I'm not lying to you."

He willed her to remember and begged the gods to break whatever spell the witch had placed on her to block her memories of him.

"I'm sorry. I ... I just don't remember you or any of it. I remember going camping. I spent the weekend alone," she said.

"You didn't. I was there with you. I watched you set up your tent. You knew that I was watching you and called me out. The connection we had was immediate and undeniable. What happened between us that weekend was magical. We completed the mating ritual."

"Oh!" Allie said. "I don't know what to say."

"Tell me you believe me," he begged.

"I ... I honestly don't know what to believe. You said that I called you to my parent's house. What did I say? I don't even remember going there. I just remember Helena standing in front of me and being chained to a chair."

"Son of a bitch. I will kill all of them," he growled.

"You'll do no such thing. Those are my parents that you're talking about killing. I don't know or care what your beef is with them, but it stops here." She got right up in his face and argued to save the lives of those who sought to rip them apart.

"It's only because you don't remember what happened. You told me there was a witch holding you hostage in your old bedroom," Marc said.

"I don't remember that. What else?" she asked.

"You said that her magic was fading, and you had a plan to escape. Then you told me that you killed her and were about to leave before your parents got back from wherever they were."

"I killed someone!" Allie shouted.

"From what I understand, you did it to defend yourself."

She was clearly upset by what he had told her. "Allie, I'm sorry. I wish there was a way to make you remember."

"What else did I tell you?" she asked, shaking off his comments.

"That your parents had another witch, and they wanted to break our mating connection and make you forget about me. I should have been there to stop it. I should have never let you go there alone." Marc would have kicked his own ass if he could figure out how to make his leg move in that direction. Sadly, he couldn't, and now they had to deal with the consequences of him not being able to save her from her mom and dad.

"And Clinton? Do you know him?" she asked, seeming to take in everything that he had said.

"No. The only thing I know about him is that if he lays his hands on you again, he's going to lose those hands and a whole lot more," Marc growled, imagining how fun it would be to make the fucker pay for his part in all of this.

"Agreed," Allie said.

For once, her fury seemed to match his own.

"Marc, is it?" she asked.

"Yes."

"I don't know what to believe right now. I feel something between us. I do. It's there. But I need to figure all of this out first. I need to find out what my parents are up to and why."

"I get that, but please don't block me out of your life. Let's figure out all of this together. Besides, I don't trust that asshole, Clinton. He has some evil plan cooked up. My gut is telling me that we can't trust him ... that he's up to no good, and your parents are backing him for whatever reason," Marc said.

"I know. He's been a family friend for years. Hell, we grew up together, and I think my parents always expected that I would marry him. But there's never been any sort of spark or attraction to him at all. He's more like a cousin than anything else. He's never shown any sort of violence toward me until today. Would he have really hurt me?"

All he wanted was to wrap her in his arms and give her the comfort she so clearly needed, but he was afraid of scaring her off, and that pissed him off because she was his mate. Not that she remembered their mating, but he had to be careful. He didn't want to risk upsetting her any further than she already was.

"I wouldn't have let him hurt you. You have to know that." Marc's heart broke for Allie, and there didn't seem to be a fucking thing that he could do about it.

"I don't know why or how, but I know. I believe you. Every instinct in my body is telling me to trust you above anyone else right now."

Marc didn't care what his gut told him. He pulled Allie into his arms and held her tight. He felt her body soften against his instantly. She buried her face in his chest and cried. Scooping her up into his arms, he carried her the rest of the way to her house.

"I know I don't remember anything about you, but this feels so damn familiar," she said in between sniffles.

"I know, baby. I've got you." He gently set her on the porch and pulled her spare key from his pocket, and unlocked the door.

"How do you have the keys to my house? Never mind." She sighed.

"You gave it to me the other night," he said, scooping her back into his arms.

"This night just keeps getting weirder and weirder."

NINETEEN

ALLIE

Allie sighed again as Marc carried her into her house. He laid her on the couch and pulled the blanket hanging on the back of the couch over her shoulders. He yanked off her boots and placed them by the door where she normally kept her shoes. On the way back, he stopped by the fridge and grabbed her a bottle of water.

"Here," he said, handing her the bottle. "You need to drink something."

She gladly accepted the bottle and took a few gulps. "I think a beer would taste a hell of a lot better and probably calm my nerves more than water." She laughed.

"I'm sure it would, but for right now, we just

need to get some water and some food into you before you go into shock."

Allie stared at him, willing herself to remember anything about him. While everything about him, his voice, touch, and his mannerisms, all seemed familiar to her, he did not. "I'm going to give myself a migraine if I keep trying to remember our time together," she said.

There was a knock at the door, and Marc stood to answer it. "I'll get it. You just relax."

"Okay," she agreed, not really wanting to even know who the hell was knocking at her door.

"Is she okay?" Gerri asked as she stepped into the living room.

"Yeah. I'm okay. Just super confused right now." And that was God's honest truth. "I feel like I'm going insane," she admitted. It wasn't an exaggeration. Not at all. Marc clearly knew her. Gerri clearly knew about their relationship. Yet, Allie didn't have a fucking clue.

"I bet, honey. It sucks when you have a witch scramble your brains. It's no fun, and it's, in my opinion, the ultimate violation of you as a person," Gerri said, sitting on the chair across from her.

"Why would my parents do this to me? What do they have to gain? If what Marc says is true, he and I completed the mating ritual. Why would they break that? Why would they take my fated mate away from me?"

Allie couldn't seem to wrap her head around any of it. Yes, her parents had always had high expectations and had driven her crazy when she was growing up, but to break her fated mating. That seemed extreme even for them.

"Your parents belong to a group of fundamentalists who believe in marrying within a certain social and political circle," Gerri explained. "My guess is that they snapped when you told them about your mating to Marc. They simply couldn't allow it."

"But why drag Clinton into this? What does he have to do with all of it?" Allie asked. She didn't want to believe what Gerri had said about her parents, but she knew it was the truth. She heard it in Gerri's voice.

Not only that, her mom and dad had always been involved in setting others up and arranging marriages within the family and tiger community as a whole. The matches were always advantageous and always with prestigious families. When a girl came of age, there was always a big party to introduce her to the community.

It had been that way since Allie could remember. Even when she had come of age, her parents had thrown her a massive party where all the eligible bachelors showed up in droves. Her mom had tried to tell her that it was nothing more than a coincidence, but geez. Allie hadn't believed it then, and she sure as hell didn't believe it now.

"My belief is that Clinton was the one they had secretly betrothed you to. That you were to be his wife, his mate," Gerri said.

"Oh! No!" Allie gasped. Suddenly, everything clicked in her mind. All the dinners that her parents had set up and invited Clinton. All the questions they had about what she had thought about him and dates with him that they had tried to set her up on. Her stomach churned with the thought of her parents forcing her to marry or mate him. "What the hell are they thinking?" she asked. "I have never been interested in Clinton as a mate or husband, let alone as a boyfriend." She gagged at the thought.

"They wanted their daughter to marry into a certain family and were paid handsomely for that arrangement," Gerri said.

"I feel like I'm going to be sick," Allie said, tears slipping from her eyes.

"Hey. Hey, baby. I'm here." Marc sat beside her and pulled her into his lap.

She should have refused and pushed him away, but she just couldn't bring herself to it. He felt like her only lifeline right now. Like everything and everyone that she had ever known had some plot to get her.

Allie sank into Marc's heat. Placing her head against his chest, she listened to the sound of his heartbeat. The steady and rhythmic thump, thump calmed her frayed nerves. He was so strong and vibrant, while she felt so weak and defeated by her own damn family.

Marc ran his hand up and down her arm in a soothing motion.

"I hate how weak I feel right now," she said.

"There is nothing weak about you. The shit you've had thrown at you tonight ... the fact that you're still standing after the blatant attack on you ... Allie, you are the strongest person I know," Marc said.

"I agree. You've been dealt a shitty hand. I'd be worried if you were up and dancing around the room right now. What you're feeling is normal when the ones who are supposed to have your best interest at heart betray you in the most personal ways. I'm going to let the two of you talk things over. Marc, call me if you need anything at all." Gerri stood to leave.

"Thank you for all of your help. I know we just met, but ..." Allie said, letting her words slow to a stop.

"You have nothing to thank me for. I don't like bullies. I especially don't like bullies who go after my friends or clients." Gerri winked and left.

"She's a good one to have on our side," Marc said.

"I'm so sorry. You must think I'm certifiably insane." Allie wondered what man would want her with all this shit. It was too much. Even she knew that.

"Are you kidding? Allie, baby. You are my mate. I will be by your side no matter what. Whoever comes at you comes at me. You are my life."

Marc's words opened the floodgate of tears she had been trying like hell to hold back. He grabbed a few tissues from the box on the end table and handed them to her. Not saying another world, he held her until she passed out in his arms.

ALLIE WOKE a few hours later with Marc still holding her. "I'm sorry. I didn't mean to fall asleep on you," she said, trying to scoot off of him.

"Don't be silly," he said, holding her.

"You're a good man, Marc," she said, glancing into those stunning green eyes of his. Heat pooled in her core. His nostrils flared. She felt his erection pressing against her backside.

"Allie ..." Marc said, his voice filled with lust.

She reached up and wrapped her arms around his neck, pulling his lips down to meet hers. There absolutely was something between them, and she wanted to find out exactly what it was.

His lips closed over hers. His kiss was light at first. His lips were warm and soft and made her want so much more. She moaned into his mouth, and he took advantage of that opening to slide his tongue into her mouth.

Sweet Jesus, he poured every emotion he had into that kiss, making love, slowly and sweetly, to her mouth. His tongue slid against hers and retreated. His hands were everywhere at once, caressing and massaging every inch of her body. He knew exactly where she wanted to be touched before she even knew.

Allie was surprised by how well he knew her

body. It clearly was not the first time they had been together. She wanted to forget all about her missing memories for a bit. Or the fact that they were mates, and she just couldn't remember any of it. She wanted this big hunk of a man more than anything at that moment.

"Baby?" Marc said, but it was more of a question. Like, was she sure that she really wanted to do this ... right here and right now ...

"Yes. Please. I just want to forget all of my problems for now, and I have the feeling you could make me forget if the world was about to end."

"You're certain?" he asked again, making sure she knew what she was getting herself into.

"Absolutely," she said.

TWENTY

MARC

Marc could hardly believe that Allie wanted him, even without her memories. He had only wanted to be there to comfort her ... to help her figure out the mess they were in. He would have been happy to hold her all night long while she slept, but she had woken up wanting him.

He checked and double-checked to make sure that he was really what she had wanted, and it was. He stood with her in his arms, eliciting a squeal of delight out of her. Carrying her back to the bedroom, he pulled the comforter down and laid her on top of the sheets.

"It's so weird that you know your way around my house and know where everything is."

"I've spent a lot of time here this past week, baby. But I have to ask you one more time."

"A triple check?" she giggled.

"Exactly." He didn't want to push her into anything before she was one hundred percent ready for it. Even if they had already made love a few dozen times since they had become mates.

Allie lifted her hips and shimmied out of her jeans and underwear. "I'm positive." She sat up, pulled her sweater over her head, and threw it across the room along with her bra.

"Well, then ..." Marc kicked off his boots and ditched his jeans quicker than he would have ever thought possible. Next was his T-shirt. His cock jutted out proudly for her viewing pleasure.

She sucked in a deep breath. "Oh, my!" she chewed on her bottom lip. "If you really are my mate, then the fates truly have blessed me." She patted the bed, motioning him to join her.

She didn't have to ask him twice. He laid on his side, and his fingers danced a trail over her heavy breasts and down her stomach before working their way back up to her breasts. He cupped one at a time. Leaning over, he kissed and sucked each of her nipples, turning them into hard peaks.

"Mmm," she moaned. Her hand went straight

for his cock. She wrapped her fingers around his length and squeezed.

It took all of his willpower not to come right there in her hand. Biting the side of his cheek until he tasted blood, he willed himself to calm down. Though they had made love many, many times, he had to prove himself all over again because she couldn't remember a single second of their previous times together.

He kissed a path down the valley between her breasts to her stomach. Circling her belly button with his tongue, he dipped it inside before continuing his path to the juncture between her legs.

"Oh!" she cried out as he pushed her hips apart and slid his hand over her folds.

"You're so wet," he growled, sliding a finger into her pussy and pumping it in and out.

"I need you," she moaned.

"Soon, baby. But not before I make you come all over my face a few times." He positioned himself between her legs and pulled her thighs up over his shoulders.

"Marc!" she whimpered.

"You have such a beautiful pussy." He slid his tongue over her clit and down to her sweet hole.

"Oh!"

"And you taste so fucking good. I've said it a million times, and I'll say it a million more. You taste like the sweetest damn candy I've ever tasted." He wasn't joking. He didn't know what it was about her juices, but he was addicted to them. Flattening his tongue, he slid it up to her clit and sucked the tiny bundle of nerves into his mouth.

Her body vibrated with each swipe of his tongue. Oh, hell yeah. He knew exactly what she liked, and he was going to show her, once again, that he was the only one who could make her feel so damn good.

He licked and sucked on her clit until she tossed her head back and forth on the bed. Knowing that she was getting close to climaxing, he slid two fingers into her soaked pussy and began scissoring them in and out until she was screaming his name, and her body was shaking.

A gush of her sweet juice coated his tongue as her climax claimed her, and he lapped up every drop and wanted more. He slid a third finger into her and slowed his pace.

"Oh, God! You have my pussy so filled up. I can feel you stretching me," she moaned, twisting her hips back and forth.

"I do. I want to make sure you're ready for my

cock." He slid his tongue from her ass and back up to her entrance.

"Oh!" she gasped at his bold action.

"Does that feel good, baby?" he asked.

"So fucking good," she groaned.

"Good, because I'm going to do it again and again." He circled her ass once more. Her entire body shivered when he did it. Goosebumps broke out all across her flesh. Her pussy clenched around his fingers.

The more she seemed to get off on what he was doing, the more he licked her tight hole. Just as another climax was starting to crash over her, he slid a finger into her tightness, filling both of her holes.

"Fuck!" Allie shouted. "Marc! I ... Oh! God!"

He pulled the finger out and pushed it back in. Working both her pussy and her ass at the same time had her coming hard. She squeezed her breasts and bucked her hips against his face as her honey coated his tongue in wave after wave.

"Marc! Please! I ... I don't know how much more I can take. I feel like I'm going to fucking die!" she cried out.

"Tell me to fuck you, Allie," he growled,

pumping his fingers in and out of her pussy and ass ... not letting up for a single second.

"Yes! Yes! Oh, please! Fuck me! Now!"

"Are you sure?" he asked, slamming his fingers in and out of her holes.

"Yes! Please!"

ALLIE WASN'T sure how much more she could take. This would be the way to go if she were going to die. Of that, she had zero doubt. Never before had she had such a body-altering orgasm ... or orgasms? Well ... that she knew of anyway. For all she knew, this could just be another Tuesday night between her and Marc.

The only thing that she did know for certain was that she wanted his cock in her now. She needed to feel him slamming into her more than she needed the breath in her lungs or to see the sun come up tomorrow. It was as if she needed him on a cellular level. Like every part of her body begged for him and all the naughty things he could do to her.

"Mmm ..." Allie moaned when Marc positioned the head of his cock at her entrance.

"Are you ready for me?" he asked.

"Yes! Please do it now! Please!" She didn't care how needy she sounded. Nor did she care that she was literally begging a guy to fuck her silly.

He yanked her ankles up over his shoulders and slammed balls deep inside her with a single shift of his hips.

"Fuck!" she shouted, loving the way his thickness filled her.

"Are you okay?" he asked, holding perfectly still.

"I'm better than okay. Now move that ass and make me come all over your cock," she demanded.

"Yes, ma'am." Marc laughed.

His smile lit up his whole face before his features took on a far more serious look as he pulled his cock out to the tip and slammed back in, rocking the entire bed. "Uhh ... Damn, baby. You are always so fucking tight around my cock," he groaned, tossing his head back.

"That's because you're fucking huge," she moaned, loving every second of him stretching her to the max.

"I'm not that big. Either way, I love the way you feel. How wet you are. How tight you are." He ground his hips into her, going as deep as he possibly could.

"Fuuuck, yes!" she moaned, her fangs punching through her gums, and she knew her eyes were glowing.

"There's my mate. So fucking hot and sexy." Marc picked up his pace and began ramming his cock in and out of her.

"Yes! Yes! Yes!" she shouted, chasing her next climax. She was so close she could practically taste it. "Make me come!" she shouted.

"Don't you worry, baby. I know exactly what you need to push you over the edge." He slipped a finger between their bodies and began to rub her clit.

"Oh! Yes! That's it! Don't stop! Please! Don't stop fucking me!" She panted as white lights danced in her vision. Every nerve ending in her body kicked into high gear at the same time.

"Don't worry, baby. I have no intentions of stopping anytime soon," he said, leaning over, licking her nipples before taking turns and sucking each one into his mouth.

"Good," she cried out, arching her back off the bed. "I need more!"

Marc pulled out and flipped her over onto her

stomach before pushing her legs apart with his knees. "I need to taste you one more time," he said, bending down and running his tongue from her clit up to her ass, pausing to circle her tight hole.

"Oh, God! Marc! That feels so damn good," she purred, turning her head to the side.

"Does it make you nervous when I do this?" he asked.

"It should, but it doesn't. I know I can trust you to never hurt me. I don't know how I know that, but I do. Every instinct in my body keeps telling me to surrender to you in all ways possible."

Oh, how he loved hearing those words coming from her mouth. "I promise to never hurt you. I'll only make you feel amazing things. Things you never thought possible," he said, licking a path over her cheeks and up the small of her back.

He rubbed his cock over her folds and pressed slowly into her pussy. She was so tight in this position he had to fight back his urge to blow his seed in her. The way her pussy squeezed his cock with each thrust was driving him fucking wild. He pulled out to the tip and palmed his cock. It was covered in Allie's sweet honey. Slowly he ran the tip up to her tiny back hole and pressed it into her.

"Ohhh," she moaned.

"Am I hurting you?" he asked. The last thing he wanted was to cause her any pain. This was supposed to be all about pleasure.

"No. It feels so, so good. I had no idea it could feel like this." She pushed her backside against him, trying to get him to go deeper.

"Easy, baby. We need to do this slowly, or you're going to regret it." He pushed another inch of his length into her ass.

"I trust you," she moaned.

"Your ass feels so damn good around my cock." He pressed in a bit farther before coming to a stop and letting her adjust to his cock filling her ass.

"More! Please!" she begged.

He kissed and nipped at her back and shoulder before burying the rest of his cock in her tight hole.

"Yes!" she moaned. "Oh, Marc. I ... I'm going to come like this. The pressure is incredible."

"Not yet, baby. Hold it for now. I promise it will make it all the more worth it when you do finally come." He reached around to her clit and began a series of slow, laconic circles designed to drive her insane and give her the boost she needed to fly over the edge and into the abyss with her climax.

TWENTY-ONE

ALLIE

Allie could hardly believe the pleasure Marc was giving her. Damn, if anyone would have ever told her that she'd enjoy having a cock in her ass, she would have laughed it off and called them crazy, but here she was, begging Marc to fuck her ass even harder than the pounding he was already giving her.

"God, baby," he groaned, pulling out to the tip and slamming back into her ass.

"Yes! Please, Marc! Give it to me," she shouted, bucking her hips back to meet each of his forceful thrusts.

"Yes! Yes!" he joined in her shouting. "Fucking, damn, baby!"

"I'm going to come, Marc, and I want you to come with me this time. Please," she begged.

"Are you sure?" he asked.

"I'm positive! Now come with me, damn it."

Those were Allie's last coherent words before yet another climax swept her away, mind, body, and soul. She felt as if she were floating through the stars, reaching for some unknown entity ... or the missing puzzle pieces in her mind. Allie wouldn't have had a care in the world if she had floated away into the great unknown as long as she had Marc with her and the pleasure that he gave her never stopped.

"Uh! Fuck!" Marc groaned, pumping his hips once, twice, before his seed jetted deep into her ass, and he slowed his hurried thrusts.

Allie panted for air. Her lungs were burning from the effort. It felt like she had run a fifty-mile race. Marc rolled off her and dragged her onto her side, snuggling against her. He covered her shoulder and the back of her neck with a thousand kisses. All the while praising her.

"You are the most amazing woman I've ever met."

"Is that code for thank you for the amazing roll

in the sack?" she joked, needing to lighten the mood.

"Oh, yes, but so much more," he said.

"Yeah? Care to clue me in?" she asked.

"Hold that thought for a moment," Marc said, hopping out of bed and heading for the attached bathroom.

Watching him walk across the room and the way his ass swayed, man, she'd drop a buck in a machine for that view any day. The man truly was sex on legs. She would fight anyone who dared to disagree. And fuck, he was talented, to boot. He'd given her more orgasms than she'd ever had in a single night, and by the looks of things, he was nowhere near done with her.

Fine by me, she thought.

She heard the cabinet open, and the water turn on. After a few seconds, he returned with a damp washcloth and a dry towel.

"Here, let's get you cleaned up a bit," he said, gently running the washcloth between her legs, followed by the dry towel.

"Mmm," she moaned as his fingers lingered on her folds, teasing her just slightly. Though he had just given her countless orgasms, she was already primed and ready for more. Allie didn't know if it was Marc that had made her so wanton and feral or if it was something instinctual, but with him, she had zero inhibitions. Like nothing was off the table when it came to the pleasure he could give her. She wanted all of it. No questions asked.

"Do you want more, baby?" he asked, continuing to tease her.

"I want all of it. Everything you have to offer," she purred, stroking his length until he was rock hard once again.

"That sounds like a tall order. It could take me a while to show you all of my tricks ... an entire lifetime."

"I just might like the sound of that. Especially if you keep giving me so many orgasms."

"Baby, I'm full of orgasms, and they all have your name on them." He nipped at her lips as he slid two fingers back into her pussy. "You are absolutely soaked." He sucked in a gasp.

"I am, and it's all for you. I want more, Marc. Do you think you're up for it?" she asked with the shyest smile she could muster.

He palmed his cock and pumped his thick length up and down inches from her face. "Does it look like I'm up for round two, baby?" he asked, his voice filled with lust.

"Uh-huh. It sure does." She ran a finger down her stomach to her folds and began circling her clit. Watching him stroke his cock was the hottest thing she had ever witnessed.

"You like watching me?" he asked, his eyes studying every movement she made like a hawk.

"I do. It's hot. Ohh," she let out a soft moan.

"I'm glad you think so."

"I want to taste you," she said, running her tongue over her lips.

"Do you?" He teased her by moving slightly closer to her.

"I do." She wondered if he would taste as good as he looked. Marc lay on the bed and pulled her hips over his face. "How about we taste each other?" He pulled her pussy down onto his face.

"Yes!" she purred, sliding her tongue from the tip of his cock clear down to the base and back up. She lifted his heavy cock with her hand before closing her mouth over the tip. His sweet and salty taste drove her wild. She pumped her face up and down, swallowing as much of his length as she could without making herself choke.

"Fucking hell! You are good at that. So damn good!"

"Actually, I've never been a fan of it ... until

now. There's something about this beautiful cock of yours that makes me want to do this." She closed her mouth around his cock again. This time, she pumped her hand up and down in unison, working his entire cock at the same time. Squeezing his sac with the other hand, she rocked her hips up and down on his face, loving the way his tongue hit her in the right spot every time.

She moaned on his cock with each swipe of his tongue across her clit. "Marc!" Wiggling her hips against his face, he gripped her hips and began to fuck her with his tongue. She nearly shot out of her skin when he pulled back and nipped her ass.

"Hey!" she laughed.

"My cock needs to be inside that tight pussy of yours, now!" he growled.

"I agree!" She quickly spun around and straddled his waist.

"Now, isn't this a sight for sore eyes," he said, reaching up and caressing her breasts.

"Am I?" she asked as she palmed his cock and began to lower herself down onto him.

"Indeed." He sucked in a deep breath when he was fully seated deep inside her. "God, baby."

"I know, right? I don't think I'll ever get tired of this feeling. How good it feels every time I have you filling me. You said we completed the mating ritual the first time we had sex?" she asked, grinding herself onto his cock, taking him as deep as possible.

"The second time," he groaned.

"I think I know why." She giggled.

"Oh, yeah? Care to share?"

"Because of how good you feel inside me." She lifted her hips and dropped quickly down to his. He grabbed onto her sides, steadying her on his cock.

"So it's all about my dick?" He laughed.

"No. Not quite, but damn, it certainly is a huge, huge bonus."

"I'm really glad you think so." Marc lifted her by her hips and dropped her down onto his cock.

"God, and that feels so fucking good," Allie purred. She pumped her hips up and down in a round motion, loving the way the head of his cock felt each time it pressed against her most sensitive spot.

"I love it when you ride my cock like this, baby. It's so fucking hot to watch your tits bounce and to feel your pussy gripping me so damn tight."

"I see how it is. You just want me for my

pussy," she teased, leaning down and nipping at his chest.

"Hell, no, baby. But it is a tight, tight, reason as to why you might think that," he said, rolling her over onto her back and quickly plunging back into her balls deep.

"Oh, God! Yes! Fuck me, Marc!" she shouted as he slammed into her harder and faster. The headboard slammed against the wall with each thrust.

"It's a good thing I don't have neighbors." She giggled as he slowed his pace to catch his breath.

"We would put on one hell of a show if you did."

Marc stretched his muscles out over her, lifting her hands above her head. He twisted his hips with each glide of his cock in and out of her heat. She loved the way the rim of his head felt each time he pulled out and pushed through her tight entrance. The muscle that stretched to accommodate his width was getting one hell of a workout.

She wrapped her legs around his back and locked her ankles in place as she raced toward her next climax. "Marc, I'm so damn close. Please, please, push me over the edge before I go insane from needing to come," she begged.

The way he moved and how each thrust felt had her soaring to new heights quicker than she would have ever thought possible. Sex with Marc was like nothing she had ever experienced in her entire life. Of that, she was entirely certain. Allie couldn't imagine it getting any better than here and now.

"That's it, baby. I want you to come all over my cock. I need to feel you squeezing so tight around me. I want to feel you milking my seed out of my cock with your pussy," Marc groaned.

"Oh! Yes! That's it! Just like that! Oh! Oh!" Allie couldn't hold back any longer and wouldn't have been able to, even if she had tried. With that one last twist of his hips, he sent her rushing headlong into a frenzy of pleasure.

Her entire body shook to the point that the bed vibrated under her like a quarter bed at a cheap motel. She tossed her head from side to side and scored his back with her nails. Thankfully, they were both shifters, and the blood she was sure she was drawing from the cuts would stop quickly with his shifter healing.

Her inner walls clamped down around his length, and she watched as he gritted his teeth, trying to hold back. "Come for me, please!" she begged.

"God, baby!" Marc pumped his hips once more, then jetted his hot seed deep inside her pussy.

"Mmm," she purred as he collapsed on top of her. Running her fingers through his messy hair, she thought that this was absolute heaven on earth. She couldn't think of a single time in her entire life when she'd felt such a pure and simple peace with everything around her.

Even with all the chaos in her life, the betrayal of her parents, and one of her closest friends, at this moment, Allie knew that Marc belonged to her as much as she belonged to him. She didn't need her tiger to tell her, nor did she need the fates to intervene or to save her from what was to come. She knew in the depths of her heart that they belonged together.

"Penny for your thoughts, baby?" Marc scooted off to the side and pulled her into his arms.

"I'm just thinking about how perfect this feels," she said, opting for honesty.

"That's a very good description," he said with a smile. "The only small thing I wish was different was that you had your memories. I wish you could remember we were mates, and we were happy. I was too happy to have you in my life."

"I want back what they took from me. I want those memories we made together. I need those memories so I can be whole again. So I can remember everything," she said. Allie no longer doubted that her parents had taken away her memories of Marc. It really was the only explanation that made sense.

There was too much he knew about her for them not to have known each other before their meeting at her parents' home. Not only that, but he also had the key to her house, and he knew where everything was. A stranger wouldn't know that. None of it.

If she added up all those things, plus the conversation she'd had with Gerri, she could easily piece together what had happened. Though she may have questioned the story when she first heard it from Marc and Gerri, she knew without a doubt that it was the absolute truth.

Neither of them had any reason to lie to her. Not only that, she could hear the truth in their words, the conviction with which they had spoken. And she had heard the falsehoods spewing from her dad's mouth. That was something that had rocked Allie to her core.

"Right now, we need to get some rest. It's been a long day. Tomorrow is another day, and we will figure out how to get your memories back. I promise, baby. If it's the last thing I do." Marc turned off the lights and pulled the blankets up over them. He wrapped her in his arms and held her tight.

She let out a soft sigh before drifting off to sleep with more love in her heart than she had ever known.

TWENTY-TWO

MARC

Marcus combed his fingers through Allie's hair as she slept peacefully, curled up in his arms. Her eyes slowly started to flutter open, and a smile spread across her face.

"Good morning, baby. I was wondering when I'd see those beautiful eyes of yours or if you were going to sleep the day away." His heart felt full with his mate snuggling next to him. Even if she couldn't remember, she was his mate.

"What time is it?" she asked.

"A little after eight. It's still pretty early, but I've been awake for a while thinking about everything," he said.

"So serious first thing in the morning. Let's get

some coffee in us, and then we can talk about what's on your mind."

"That sounds like one hell of a plan."

"Good, I'll start the coffee. You can hit the shower first."

"Another great idea."

"I seem to be full of them today, and the day is just starting." She giggled.

Marc watched as Allie grabbed a robe and a pair of slippers and made her way out to the kitchen. Damn, he really was a lucky guy, and the fates truly had blessed him. Hopping out of bed, he headed for the shower, looking forward to the hot water soaking into his muscles.

After a few minutes, he joined Allie in the kitchen. "I think I've come up with a way to get some of your memories back," Marc said, carefully observing her reaction.

Allie tilted her head, curious as to what he had come up with, but she sensed his idea came with a caveat. "You seem almost reluctant to suggest it. Why?" she asked, pouring the steamy java into his cup and handing it to him.

"For one, it involves going to see a witch." After yesterday's debacle, he wasn't sure how she would feel about dealing with any more witches. Hell, he really didn't like the idea of it either, but what choice did they really have when it came down to it? Allie wanted her memories back. What better way?

"Okay, but you realize my father's witch would never agree to cross him and restore my memories." She looked at him as if he had grown a second tail.

"Yeah, I know, but this is a different witch and someone I know and trust. Her name is Gabby, and she has no connection to your father or his witch. Would you be willing to trust her too?" Marcus really hoped that she would agree to his plan because he wanted her memories to come back to her as well.

He hated the fact that her parents were the kind of people who would do something like this. It would certainly make the family gatherings awkward. When it came down to it, it pissed him off and made him want to exact revenge on the people responsible for causing his mate any type of pain.

"I'm willing to take your word for it. However, I hate to break it to you, but only my father's witch can return my memories. And I doubt that's happening."

"That's the other part of what I want to tell

you. They wouldn't exactly be your memories, but mine. I think Gabby can copy my memories and transfer them to you. Memories of how we met and our time together. These are shared memories. The only difference is that they would be from my perspective."

His plan sounded stupid now that he said it out loud. He didn't know what the hell he'd been thinking when the idea had popped into his head. It wasn't a perfect solution, but considering the circumstances, he figured it was the best they could come up with. And far better than doing nothing. He watched her silently process the plan.

"This requires a huge leap of faith on my part. You know that, right? I mean, how do I know you wouldn't collude with your witch to fill my mind with false memories? I mean, if you intend to trick me or play me in any way, it would be the perfect way to do it."

"All I can do is ask you to trust me, Allie. Trust me. I know you feel the bond between us. It's real. And by giving you my memories, you'll finally be able to make sense of what this is between us. Wouldn't that be worth taking a chance on?"

"I ... I guess so. It's just ..."

"Listen, there's a way to do this where you can trust me."

"How?" she asked.

"If at any point you decide this plan of mine doesn't seem to feel right, we'll reverse everything. What do you say?"

Allie got up and paced two laps around the room. Finally, she stopped to look him in the eye. "Knowing that I've had my memories erased, it's like losing a part of my life, of who I am. And knowing we have a past, but without any context ... it leaves a giant hole in my soul. So, my answer is yes. It will be worth it to at least try."

"Great. I'll call Gabby and tell her we're on our way," Marc said, resisting the urge to pick her up and kiss her right there, knowing that if they got started again, they'd spend all day in bed. Instead, he politely nodded and made the call.

Within minutes, they had finished their coffee and dressed, and now he was steering his truck onto the seldom-traveled backroads on the edge of town where the street signs no longer guided their way through the fog. A small one-story house, nearly concealed by garden beds that were so overgrown they seemed more like little patches of jungle, came into view.

Taking Allie by the hand, they followed a flagstone walkway that snaked through the garden and led them to the front porch. Before he could knock, the front door creaked open on its own as if the house was welcoming them.

Gabby stepped into the hallway, her tiny frame almost hidden by a planter. The little old woman was all smiles. "Welcome, Marc, come inside. And you must be Allie." She said, wrapping her in a hug.

The door slammed shut and locked itself behind them as they followed Gabby into the living room. "We can talk in here," she said, motioning for her guests to take a seat on her couch. "Marc, you told me you had a favor to ask. What is it?"

"It's really a favor for Allie. She's had certain memories removed from her mind by a witch who was acting on orders from Allie's father."

"Stop right there. You know I can't undo something like that. Only the witch who took the memories has the ability to replace them."

"I don't want you to replace her memories. You see, her father thinks he can sabotage our mating by using magic to undo our mating and erase any memories that Allie has of me, of us together. I was hoping you could tap into my memories and share them with her."

"Allie, is this something you agree with? I must know if you consent to this before I even attempt it," Gabby said.

"I don't think I have a choice, to be honest. I need to know what happened between us."

Gabby shrugged. "Then I'll do it."

"Are there any risks we should know about?" Marc asked.

"The only risk is if it turns out Allie is disappointed in what she sees. But I hardly think that will be the case."

"What do we have to do?"

"It's fairly simple. Just follow my instructions. Turn, face each other, and just relax. Close your eyes and take deep breaths and slowly let them out," she said, placing a hand on top of each of their heads.

"All right, Allie. I need you to clear your mind of everything. Imagine that you are standing alone in an empty field, and it's perfectly quiet. Marc, I want you to remember the first moment you set eyes on Allie. Allow yourself to examine every detail. Then slowly unroll all of your memories of her. Let them flow. It's fine if they get out of order, they will sort themselves out in the end. Are the two of you ready?" she asked.

Marc silently nodded, as did Allie.

For him, this was easy. He could remember every detail of the day he set eyes on her. From the way the sun was shining, the breeze in the air, to every fine detail of her delicious body.

As the memories flooded his mind, he felt a weird tingling sensation emanating from the palm of Gabby's hand. It wasn't exactly uncomfortable, but as Gabby began to recite a chant in a strange language, the intensity of the sense increased. Then it became painful.

Despite his own discomfort, all he could think about was Allie. If he could only see her. But he couldn't open his eyes. Gabby's spell left him physically paralyzed while his brain buzzed with swirling memories of Allie.

Then, almost like hitting a switch, the pain subsided. His eyes fluttered open.

"Allie?" He groaned.

And then he saw how her head hung limply with her chin on her chest. "Allie!"

Gabby staggered backward, clearly exhausted from working her magic.

Marc grabbed Allie by the shoulders, steadying

her and then cradling her in his arms. "She's unconscious. What did you do to her?"

"I did what you asked. She's only sleeping. You need to let her sleep while her mind stitches together all of your memories. This is the most important step. Hold her. Keep her comfortable. But do not, under any circumstances, try to wake her. If you do, consequences could be catastrophic for both of you."

Marc nodded. Sweeping the strands of hair from Allie's face, he relished her soft features and wished he could once again kiss her as his mate. Even though they had kissed many, many times the night before, along with several other naughty things, it wasn't the same as it was after they had completed the mating ritual.

He held her for over an hour before she began to move, and her eyes fluttered open. "Allie?"

"Wha ... what the hell? My head. Ugh, I feel like I got hit by a freight train," she said, sitting up.

"That will pass soon. Here, drink this. It's just tea, I promise. I'm going to leave you two alone for now," Gabby said, handing her a steaming mug.

"Thanks. I feel like I have a brand-new movie, all queued up and ready to watch."

"Take your time," Marc said.

Allie pulled her knees up to her chest and sipped the tea. "I don't think I can stop going over these memories. Even if I tried."

As desperate as he was to find out what, if any, memories stuck with her, he waited patiently.

"Oh my God!" she shouted.

"What's wrong?"

"Were you stalking me? Watching me like that? I mean, I knew you were there. I guess I didn't realize how taken by me you were at first."

"You think that's something. Just wait. Things are going to get spicy."

He watched her close her eyes as she viewed his memories. Before long, she squirmed, and she began to breathe rapidly. Then she gasped in both shock and pleasure.

"Oh, my God. We did that on the first day we met? I did that? What the hell?"

"I tried to warn you."

"Wow." Her face turned crimson red.

"Was that a good *wow*? Or …"

"Well, it's not a bad *wow*. It's not like you haven't had the full tour. Multiple times."

"Same goes for you."

"Definitely. Again, wow. I can't believe we

have this history," she said, her eyes sparkling devilishly over the mug.

"But how do you feel overall?"

"Like the missing parts are filling in. It's weird because it's not my own memories, but at the same time, they are. And this strange attraction, this magnetic pull I've had drawing me toward you ... it makes perfect sense to me now. We have something real, don't we?"

"Yes. What we have is very real."

TWENTY-THREE

ALLIE

"I can tell you're deep in thought over there. Care to share with the class?" Marc asked as he steered his truck into her driveway.

"I'm thinking that I'm glad that I agreed to go see Gabby with you, but at the same time, I'm really upset because I'm still missing my version of our story. I want those memories back, Marc. I know that only Helena can restore those memories. I have to find a way to get them back. I don't know what it's going to take, but there has to be a way. There just has to be," she said.

Allie wasn't sure what she had expected from Gabby or if Marc's plan would even be successful. She had definitely gotten more than she had bargained for, that's for sure. She was glad to know what they shared was real, even if she had been temporarily embarrassed by her wanton behavior.

How she had reacted to their first meeting definitely wasn't her normal reaction to guys. She'd never slept with a guy within hours of meeting him and certainly had never thought of herself as one who would jump into a lifelong commitment in less than twenty-four hours after meeting the person, but she clearly had with Marc.

It wasn't that she didn't believe his memories. She did. She absolutely did. What she wanted to know was *why* she had reacted to him the way she did. What had her thought process been?

She may have had the memories, or his version of them, but there were still so many questions floating around in her mind. She wanted that knowledge back, and there was only one way to get it. She had to confront her parents, and somehow, she had to talk them into getting Helena to restore her memories. It was not just Marc's version of what had happened, even if she was quite happy to know how things had gone down between them.

The idea of never remembering her version of what had truly happened between them didn't sit well. She felt like she had been robbed by her parents and Helena, and if she were being perfectly honest, Clinton. She absolutely hated how the entire situation made her feel. Gerri had been right when she said it was a violation. That was exactly how she felt. Like she'd been desecrated. And she didn't like it. Not one bit. The anger inside her bubbled to new heights.

"What do you have in mind?" Marc asked.

"I'm not sure yet. Part of me wants to storm right over to my parents' house to confront them, but I know that's not the wisest choice and would likely lead nowhere good ... especially after the bullshit they pulled last night. I can't trust them. As much as it hurts to admit the truth, it is what it is.

"They broke my trust when they violated my mind to destroy and erase our relationship. I don't know if I will ever be able to forgive them for that." Allie's chest ached. Her heart was splitting in two. She didn't know how to reconcile what had happened. The people who had given her life, who were supposed to love and protect her, had turned on her, and that awareness alone stung like a bitch.

"I think confronting your parents would be the worst option possible. Is there any way to get a hold of the witch, Helena?" he asked.

Allie shrugged. "She can't be that hard to find, can she?"

"When you put it like that ..." He smiled back at her.

"My thoughts exactly. I say we get in the house and start doing some good detective work. With any luck, we'll be able to track her down quickly so I can get my memories back and tell my parents to fuck off. Forever."

"I like the way you think."

A FEW HOURS LATER, they were exactly where they had started ... with absolutely zero information about the witch. Marc had called several of his friends, and not a single one of them knew of a witch named Helena. Several of his friends had also checked with local covens, and they all came back with the same thing. Nada.

Allie's frustrations were growing by the second. How the hell was she supposed to get her memories back if she couldn't find the witch who took them to begin with?

"Let's take a break, baby, and go get some food. There's a great little diner right around the corner from my house that serves breakfast all day long. I don't know about you, but I could put away some pancakes right about now," Marcus suggested.

"Pancakes would be good. I'm not gonna lie."

"Perfect! Race you to the truck."

"You're on!" She giggled as she jumped up off the couch, beating him to the front door. She twisted the handle, yanked the door open, and ran into a hard body blocking her path.

Before Allie could get a look at her visitor, Marc let out a ferocious roar and quickly pulled her behind him. She peeked around his shoulder and gasped in shock when she saw who it was that stood in her door frame.

"Clinton!" she shouted. "What the fuck are you doing here?" Allie growled at her former friend.

"Allie ... can we talk?" he asked, eyeing up Marc.

"Absolutely not," Marc growled at Clinton.

"I asked the lady. Not you." Clinton looked down at Marc like he was nothing more than a piece of dog shit that he had stepped in by accident.

If Allie would have blinked, she would have missed how quickly Marc did a double tap with his fist against Clinton's face. Her previous self would have been angry with Marc for going to violence right out of the gate, but that was well before Clinton had betrayed her and helped her parents commit a crime against humanity.

Clinton stumbled out of the doorframe, but he'd managed to make a quick recovery, even with the blood dripping down his face. She pushed Marc out of the way to face Clinton.

"You have some fucking nerve showing up at my doorstep after the bullshit you and my parents put me through last night. I suggest you leave before I rip your fucking throat out myself," she growled.

"Allie, love. You can't possibly mean that. We only want what's best for you," Clinton said.

"Really!" she screeched like a banshee on the warpath. "You don't get to say that to me anymore, and furthermore, how the fuck do you know what's best for me? Do you really think helping my parents break my connection to my fated mate is what's best for me? Are you fucking kidding me right now?"

Allie was livid. She couldn't believe that Clinton had the balls to show up at her doorstep, claiming that he only wanted what was best for her. His audacity blew her mind.

"You know your parents always wanted us to be together. They planned for us to be married. Then you go and mate with this ..." Once again, he eyed Marc up and down with a less-than-favorable expression on his face. "I was going to propose to you last night, and your parents knew that. They simply couldn't believe that you had run off and mated the first guy you found. What's so special about this one anyway?" Clinton asked.

"He's my mate. He's the one I will marry. The one I will spend this life and the next with. The one I'll grow old with. The one I will be buried next to. I don't know why you people don't seem to understand any of this. But that's not really my problem. I'm an adult, and I don't need to explain my decisions to anyone, let alone you.

"I have never once in my life given you a single indication that I was interested in you or that I would even accept a proposal from you. I don't know what deal you cooked up with my parents, but I'll have no part in it. So, you best be on your way. Ask my parents for a refund because I will never, ever be with you."

Allie didn't know how she could make her position any clearer than she just did. She didn't care if she hurt Clinton's feelings. And she certainly didn't give a flying fuck if her parents didn't agree with her or her decisions. It was her life to live. Not theirs. Never theirs.

"You don't know what you're saying," Clinton said, trying to argue with her.

When Allie failed to be bargained with and failed to listen to Clinton's bullshit, he reached for her, trying to yank her out of her house.

Epic. Mistake.

Marc was on him instantly. His fists flew in rapid succession, one after another, beating Clinton to a pulp.

"Do not ever, ever lay your hands on my mate again, or I will end you. Do you understand me, you piece of shit?"

Clinton nodded and stumbled back toward his Lexus. And the look he gave Allie told her he was not done with their conversation. As far as she was concerned, he no longer existed. He was dead to her. It didn't matter what he wanted to say to her; she didn't want to hear it. There was nothing he could say or do that would ever make her change her mind. She pulled Marc back inside her house and slammed the door.

"You should probably wash your hands to get the blood off before we go anywhere. I'm afraid you may have ruined your shirt as well. I have some T-shirts in my drawer, but I doubt they'd be big enough to fit you." She laughed, imagining him squeezing his large body into one of her pink T-shirts.

"No worries. We can swing by my house for a few minutes, and I can change."

"Perfect." Allie glanced out of the front window to make sure Clinton had left. She pulled her cell phone from her pocket and unlocked the screen. She had at least three dozen messages from her parents that she had no intention of reading and one from Gerri.

"Is everything all right?" Marc asked.

"Yep. I have no desire to read all the messages from my parents. They can go to hell, as far as I'm concerned. There is a message here from Gerri asking how we're doing."

"You should tell her to meet us at The Hole in The Wall for pancakes," Marc said.

"Is that really the name of the diner?" Allie laughed. Her fingers flew across her screen as she sent the invite to Gerri.

"I kid you not. Now let's get a move on before you have any more unexpected visitors."

TWENTY-FOUR

ALLIE

After a quick stop at Marc's house for him to change his clothes, they arrived at the diner. Gerri stood outside, waiting for them.

"Sorry it took us so long to get here," Marc said. "We had to run to my house. I didn't want to go running around town covered in blood."

"Oh, my! Are you all right, dear?" Gerri asked.

"I'm perfectly fine. Thanks for asking."

"Then why were you covered in blood and needing to change your clothes?"

"As we were leaving Allie's house, Clinton ran into my fists a few dozen times," Marc explained.

"Alrighty, then. That will do it. Considering he

definitely deserved it and more." Gerri held the door open for them.

"I most certainly agree." Allie smiled and headed into the diner.

She hit the brakes the second she glanced at the corner booth. Marc slammed into her back, not realizing she had stopped.

"Well, I'll be damned," Allie said as she saw the person they'd been trying to track down sitting in the booth all by her lonesome.

Allie didn't hesitate, not for a second. She marched over to the booth and sat her ass down. Marc slid into the booth beside Helena, and Gerri took the seat next to Allie.

Helena looked up in surprise as they quickly surrounded her. She was a trapped pirate ship with nowhere to go.

"If you even so much as try to utter a single syllable of a spell, I will snap your neck right here in the diner. Do I make myself clear?" Marc asked.

Helena nodded.

"You're just the person we were looking for," Allie said.

"Look, girl. I don't want no trouble with you. Your dad paid me to do a job, and I did it. If you've got a beef, it's with him. Not me."

"Oh, I agree. I definitely have a beef with my father and my mother, but also with you. You took something for me, and I want it back," she growled.

"And we'll even pay you for it," Marc said.

"And what are you two plannin' on paying me? I'm pretty sure you don't have the money lying around that the mayor has," Helena replied.

"We have something far more important." Allie smiled at Helena.

"Really, child? What's that?"

"You give me my memories back, and you get to leave with your life. I'd say it's a pretty even trade, wouldn't you?" Allie was not about to let Helena dictate the terms of how this was going to go down. The witch could either give her memories back, or she could die. It really was as simple as that.

"Well, when you put it like that, I guess we better get this show on the road. I've got people expecting me today and things to do," Helena said.

"If you try any funny stuff at all, you won't have to worry about Allie killing you. You'll be dead before you even know what happened," Marc said, warning the witch.

"Damn. You people need to chill. All this

violence isn't healthy for anyone. Now, child, give me your hand."

"Stealing one's memories isn't healthy for anyone," Allie returned the barb.

"Touché," the witch said and held out her hand.

Allie reached across the table and placed her palm in the witch's upturned hand.

Helena began to chant quietly, not wanting to draw attention from the other customers in the diner. Allie felt her palm warm as the witch's magic entered her body. She closed her eyes as a rush of images of her and Marc filled her mind.

"There! It's done. Now, if you'll excuse me, I was just leaving." Helena motioned for Marc to get the hell out of her way so she could leave, but Marc kept his ass planted in the booth until he knew for certain Allie was okay and her memories had been returned to her.

"You'll wait just a minute. I'll let you go when my mate tells me she's good. And only then."

"My patience is running low with you bossy-ass shifters," Helena snapped at him.

"Awesome! Because I've been ready to rip your throat out since I sat next to you. So, you can either chill out for a minute, or I can go home and change my clothes again because ripping your head off comes with a hella' lotta blood."

Helena zipped her mouth and waited patiently for Allie to nod that she was okay. Then and only then did Marc slide out of the booth and out of her way.

"I really hope to never see you all again. I truly mean that," Helena said.

"Ditto," Marc replied.

Sitting in the booth, Marc pulled Allie's hand into his. "Are you okay, baby? Talk to me?" he said.

"I'm just taking it all in. All of the memories. I feel like I'm whole again. I remember everything that happened between us."

"That's great news!" Gerri cheered.

Allie should've been happy. In her mind, she knew that. But it wasn't just her memories of her and Marc that Helena had returned. Oh, no.

"What's the matter, babe?" Marc asked.

"Helena returned a lot more than just the memories of you and me together," she said.

"Is that a bad thing?" he asked.

"Not at all, but it is more like a ... *I'm going to kill all of them* thing."

"Your parents? Clinton?" Marc asked. "I'm

assuming you're remembering everything that happened while you were at their house."

"Every. Single. Thing. The worst part is that I don't know how to make sure that this never happens again. How do I stop my parents from being the monsters they are?" she asked.

She would never have believed what her parents did to her without having her memories back. The true depravity of what they had done was astounding, even to her.

Allie had been lost in thought as the waitress approached their table. "Sorry, I didn't see y'all sitting here sooner. What can I get for ya?"

They rambled off their orders, and she quickly jotted them down. "I'll be right back with your drinks."

"Thanks," Gerri replied.

Allie didn't say much while they waited for their food to arrive. She listened to the back-and-forth conversation between Marc and Gerri. They were trying to plot ideas to put a stop to her parents' evil ways. As far as Clinton went, she regretted not letting Marc kill him when they had the chance.

The only thing she knew for certain about him was that his entire personality was nothing more than an act, a facade. The things he had done to her and said to her that night at her parents' house left her speechless. She had never once seen that vicious side of him in all their years of friendship.

It was amazing that he had managed to keep that part of himself so well hidden for so long. Not many people had the ability to hide themselves so completely from those they were close to.

She was thankful that Marc and Gerri kept each other company while they ate. She scarfed down her food, knowing she'd need the strength if she was going to confront her parents. And that was exactly what she had planned on doing. She just didn't know how she was going to get Marc and Gerri to agree to her plans.

Once they were finished eating, Allie cleared her throat. It was now or never. "I've come up with a plan to take down my parents for what they've been up to all these years."

"I'm all ears, babe," Marc said. "Tell me what needs to be done, and I'll gladly do it."

"I'm glad you're so agreeable. Just remember your words when I'm done talking," she said with a smile.

"ABSOLUTELY NOT! Have you lost your damn mind, woman?" Marcus was completely livid that Allie thought he would agree to her crazy plan. "There is no way I'm letting you march in there alone to face your twisted parents," he whisper-shouted, trying not to draw attention to their table. The last thing they needed was for anyone at the diner to get wind of Allie's plan and for it to get back to her dad.

"Look, I'm the only one who can do this. Neither of you will ever have a chance of making it past their guards. You know that. I have to be the one to stop them. As much as you hate my plan, you know there's no other way to do this. We have to end this here and now. We can't ever let them do this to another girl."

Allie meant every word of what she had said. Her parents were psychotic and immoral, and she couldn't let them continue to sell girls off to the highest bidders and call it making the perfect arranged marriages. Her plan would work. She didn't doubt it. She just needed to get Marc to go along with it.

"I have a high-ranking friend in the state police department," Gerri offered. "Let me call him and have him help us out. He's another shifter, so if anyone can help, it will be him." Gerri pulled her phone from her purse and scrolled through her contacts until she found the name she was looking for. Pressing the Call button, she brought the phone up to her ear and waited for her friend to answer. When he did, Gerri quickly filled him in on the plan. A few yeses and uh-huhs later and Gerri clicked the End button.

"He'll be here in ten minutes."

"Seriously! That's awesome!" Allie said.

"I still don't like it," Marc growled under his breath.

"I get that. I really do. But I can't move on with my life until this is done. And trust me when I say I want nothing more than to redo our mating ritual and spend the rest of my life with you."

"Well, when you put it like that, how can I possibly refuse?"

"Exactly."

TWENTY-FIVE

ALLIE

Allie wondered for the hundredth time what the hell she was doing and why she ever thought she could pull off this ridiculous plan of hers. She tried like hell not to fidget with the wire taped to her chest as she lifted her hand to ring the doorbell. She sucked in a deep breath and reminded herself to stay calm. This was all her idea. It was the one shot she had, and she couldn't fuck it up.

Her mother answered the door, surprised to see her standing there. "What are you doing here? Haven't you already ruined things enough for us?" her mother asked.

"We need to talk. Now!" Allie pushed her way

past her mother and entered the house. Her father stood next to the fireplace, talking to Clinton.

"Have you finally come to your senses and decided to ditch the loser?" Clinton asked.

She ignored the rude question, knowing he was only trying to goad her. She couldn't lose focus. This was too damn important. There were too many lives riding on her ability to keep her head clear and her mind focused on the task at hand.

"Allie, what are you doing here?" her father asked.

"How much did he pay you?" she asked.

"What do you mean? How much did who pay me?" her dad replied.

"Clinton. How much did he pay you?"

"I don't know what you're talking about," Alonzo said.

"Let me put it like this then ... How much was I worth to you? How much did you agree to sell me for, Dad?"

"Clearly, more than you were worth to sully yourself with the trash you decided to run off and mate with," Clinton remarked.

She really wished, once again, that she would have let Marc kill him.

"How much was it? A thousand? Five thousand? Tell me?" She persisted with her question. She wasn't giving up until she had an answer. It was more than that. She needed them to tell her exactly what went down and how much money her parents had accepted. Only then would she have what she needed.

"You think I'm that cheap?" Clinton scoffed. "That I wouldn't pay top dollar for a premium mate? Please." How she had ever thought he was a nice guy was beyond her. The man was an absolute asshole and completely beyond redemption.

"So tell me then, Clinton. How much did you pay my parents for me?" Every second that ticked by, every evaded answer, pissed her off even more. Her patience was wearing thin.

"A half million dollars."

Her mouth popped open in surprise as soon as the words left his mouth. "You gave my parents five hundred thousand dollars to ensure that I'd marry you?" She was stunned, never expecting a figure that high or ridiculous.

"Well, I figured a lifetime of breeding several children and my pretty, little wife at home waiting on me hand and foot. It would have been worth every penny that I'd spent."

Ugh! Now, she wished she'd never asked in the

first place. Every word that came out of his mouth dropped her opinion of him lower and lower. He was at rock bottom when she walked through the door. Whatever came below rock bottom, like ten levels below rock bottom, was where Clinton currently resided in her mind.

"So, that's what you do, Dad? You sell women off to the highest bidder?" she asked.

"Please!" Her mother rolled her eyes. "You act like this hasn't been done since the beginning of time. How else do you expect us to live in such luxury when your father is a politician? It's not like a small-town mayor makes any real money. Only connections. Really, you can't be that dumb."

Allie shook her head in disbelief. "I can't believe that you admit this so freely. Aren't you worried about your little secrets getting out?" she asked, truly stunned that her parents were this stupid. She found it quite funny that her mother accused her of being the dumb one.

"It's not like anyone's going to believe you, dear. We come from spectacular backgrounds, and your father is loved by everyone in town. No one would believe an angry trust-fund daughter if they thought daddy cut off her credit cards. They'd think you were nothing more than a spoiled little bitch looking for revenge, and we would happily agree with that story. Come to think of it, you would probably lose your job. Then what? You really think your firefighter can support you?"

"Ha! Trust-fund daughter. That's a good one. I've been supporting myself for years. Do you really think anybody will believe that bullshit? And as far as Marc goes, I already told you, I don't care how much money he has in the bank. What I care about is that he would never sell our daughter to some scumbag like Clinton."

"The shifters will believe my word and your father's word over yours any day. Why should I worry about any nasty little rumors you try to spread?"

"Oh, I don't think I'll need to say anything. I think you're right, Mom. I think people will listen to your words."

Just then, the front door crashed open. Two dozen state troopers filled the living room and kitchen, guns drawn and pointed at her parents.

"Don't move! The three of you are under arrest for prostitution, human trafficking, and being shitty people in general."

"I want our lawyer, now!" her dad shouted.

"Don't worry, Mayor. The boys at the jail will

make sure you get your call. In the meantime, you have the right to remain silent."

Allie stepped aside as the police read her parents and Clinton their rights which they didn't deserve after what they'd done. She didn't know if the charges would stick or if she would have to testify against them. Either way, once this hit the press, their little side gig would be put to a halt. And all those with whom her parents had done business would surely be outed as well. She had done what she could to make sure they were stopped, and that was all she could ask for.

Now, it was time for her to move on with the rest of her life.

TWENTY-SIX

EPILOGUE

"I don't know of any other couples who got to do the mating ritual twice." Marc laughed.

"I've never heard of it happening, but who knows? We can't be the only ones." Allie slid her hand down over the bulge in Marc's jeans. His erection strained against the zipper.

"Who cares if we are? The only thing I care about right now is burying myself balls deep inside of you." Marc nipped at her lips, his hand sliding under her skirt. He pushed her panties to the side and went straight for her sweet spot.

"What are you waiting for?" she asked in the sassiest tone she could muster.

"Is this what you want?" He slammed two

fingers deep into her wetness and scissored them in and out.

"Yes! Yes! That's exactly what I want and more," Allie cried out. She remembered everything about their mating ritual the second she had gotten her memories back. The fact that it had been broken by her parents and their witch still pissed her off. But that was a problem she and Marc were about to rectify.

Her parents may have tried to break them apart, and they might have succeeded if Marc had given up on her. But he hadn't, and she knew in her heart that he never would. That was exactly why doing the mating ritual was at the top of her To Do List.

"God, baby. You are so fucking hot and so damn wet for me. But you have entirely too many clothes on right now."

"That's an easy fix." She laughed and quickly pulled her dress over her head and tossed it onto the floor. She stepped out of her panties and quickly flicked the hook on her bra to ditch it. By the time she was done, Marc had also managed to make quick work of his clothes.

He had her on the bed and on her back in the blink of an eye. She giggled at his antics, but she didn't dare complain because it was exactly what she wanted.

"Ahh! That's so much better. You need to spend more time naked," he said as he pushed her legs apart with his knees and slammed into her.

"Oh! I think we can definitely work something out. But right now, I need you to make me yours ... again." She moaned at the sudden feeling of fullness. Every second he spent inside her, she absolutely loved. As far as Allie was concerned, there was nothing better and no better way to spend her time.

"Ask, and you shall receive, baby." Marc hitched her legs over his shoulders and picked up his pace. His thrusts came harder and faster until they were both panting for air.

"More! Marc! Please!" she begged. She was so close to her climax that she felt like her head was going to pop off her shoulders if she didn't come soon. Just when she thought he was going to send her flying over the edge, he slowed his pace.

Instead of the long, hard, fast thrusts he had been giving her, he switched it up to long, steady, and slow strokes, driving her absolutely insane. The pressure in her body built slowly with each glide of his cock deep into her channel. Her inner walls stretched around him to accommodate his thickness.

"God, baby. I love, love, love being deep inside you like this. Feeling your silky walls clinging to my cock. I don't think I've ever felt anything so amazing in all of my years. I want this. I want you every day for the rest of my life."

"Marc," she cried out, loving with gentle yet forcefulness of each of his thrusts. This slow burn inside her was such a contradiction to how they had normally made love. Usually, it was hot and heavy, with bodies slapping against each other until they were both ready to pass out. This was something altogether different. And she loved the absolute hell out of it.

"That's it, baby. Take every thick, hard inch of me slow and easy. I want you to feel everything my cock gives as it slides in and out of you. I want you to feel the head slipping out of you and pushing back in past that tight little muscle at the entrance of your pussy. I want you to know much I love that feeling and how good it feels every time I slide my cock into you." Marc nipped at her lips, massaged her breasts, and made love to her like no man had ever done.

Raw heat and pleasure flooded every inch of

her body, sending her into a spiraling oblivion. Before she knew it, she was racing closer and closer to her climax. "Oh, Marc. I'm so damn close."

"I know, baby. Soon. I promise." He growled as he nipped her earlobe and down her neck.

The goosebumps broke out across her body in anticipation of what was to come. She tilted her neck slightly to the side, waiting for him to make her his once again. He licked the path over the spot where he had previously bitten her. His fangs grazed her skin, causing her heart to skip a beat. Heat flooded her core.

The second his fangs pierced her skin, Allie flew to the heavens and quite possibly beyond. Her entire body trembled. Every move he made and every thrust as he pounded into her while his fangs were in her neck tripled her pleasure.

Her own fangs pushed through her gums. She buried them into that sweet spot on Marc's neck the second they were in place. His blood poured over her tongue and coated her throat. Just as before, stars danced in her vision, and she shot higher and higher into the heavens.

Her body broke into hundreds of pieces and came back together as a changed person. The half of her soul that she'd felt the witch, Helena, rip from her reappeared once again, making her whole. She clung to Marc for dear life, fearing that if she were to let go of him at that moment, she would lose him forever. That she would somehow be lost in the never-ending stars that floated around her.

Marc collapsed on top of her as they both gasped for breath, their bodies shaking and their limbs tangled together. Allie wouldn't want it any other way. She combed her fingers through his hair and enjoyed knowing they had once again completed the mating ritual.

"I have something for you," he said, his voice raspy from exertion.

"More than what you've already given me?" she asked.

"Yes," he said, sitting up and pulling the drawer open on the bedside table.

She gasped when she saw his fingers wrap around a small black velvet box. Tears pooled in the corner of her eyes as Marc walked around the bed and got down on one knee.

"Oh! God! Oh! God!" she whimpered. "Is this really happening?"

"It is, baby. I knew from the moment I laid my eyes on you that you were destined to be mine. As cheesy as it sounds, it was love at first sight. The moment I saw you, I saw our life flash before my eyes. I knew that no matter what, I had to be by your side. The way you look at me, your laugh, your smile, all of it. The total package.

"I could never imagine myself wanting to even look at another woman. Allie, you are my one true love and my fated mate. Would you do me the great honor of also becoming my wife?" Marc opened the box and waited patiently for her answer.

Allie jumped into his waiting arms.

The tears she had been holding back let loose and streamed down her face. She couldn't imagine ever being with anyone else. There wasn't another man that walked the planet who could hold a candle to her mate. She loved him more than she'd ever thought possible.

"Is that a yes?" he asked with a laugh.

"Yes! Yes! Hell, yes!" She laughed.

"I don't know what our future has in store for us, but what I do know is that I will spend every day of my life proving to you how much I love you and how much you mean to me. That is my vow to you. I love you so damn much, Allie."

"Oh, Marc! I love you too. With my whole heart."

ABOUT THE AUTHOR

New York Times and USA Today Bestselling Author

Hi! I'm Milly Taiden. I love to write sexy stories featuring fun, sassy heroines with curves and growly alpha males with fur. My books are a great way to satisfy your craving for paranormal romance with action, humor, suspense and happily ever afters.

I live in Florida with my hubby, our son, and our fur babies: Speedy, Stormy and Teddy. I have a serious addiction to chocolate and cake.

I love to meet new readers, so come sign up for my newsletter and check out my Facebook page. We always have lots of fun stuff going on there.

SIGN UP FOR MILLY'S NEWSLETTER FOR LATEST NEWS!
http://eepurl.com/pt9q1

Find out more about Milly here:
www.millytaiden.com
milly@millytaiden.com

ALSO BY MILLY TAIDEN

Find out more about Milly Taiden here:

Email: millytaiden@gmail.com

Website: http://www.millytaiden.com

Facebook: http://www.facebook.com/millytaidenpage

Twitter: https://www.twitter.com/millytaiden

You can find a complete list of all my books by series and reading order at my website: millytaiden.com

Made in United States
Orlando, FL
01 August 2024